THE RIGHT TOOL

AND OTHER POOR CHOICES

Words and pictures by

CRAIG FOSTER

Portland, Oregon

Buckman Publishing LLC
PO Box 14247
Portland OR 97293
buckmanpublishing.com

The Right Tool and Other Poor Choices/ Craig Foster

ISBN: 978-1-7323910-6-2
Library of Congress Control Number: 2019934168

This is a work of fiction. Names, characters, places, and incidents either are the products of the author's imagination or are used fictitiously. Any resemblance to actual persons, living or dead, businesses, companies, events, or locales is entirely coincidental.

Book design by Grace M.

The following stories were previously published:

"Ursa Minor" in *Tahoma Literary Review*; "The Hot Box," "Tokyo Free Time," and "Checking Out" in *Buckman Journal*; "→PDX" in *Arq Press*; and "Idol" in *1001 Journal*.

"The Right Tool" won best short story of the Attic Institute's Winter 2016 "Unrepentant" writing competition, and "Party" (then titled "Participant") won the April 2018 Mini Sledgehammer competition.

Greetings from Portland, Oregon

For The R,
Striker,
Jonty,
and Applescales

CONTENTS

Ursa Minor   1

A Little More West   5

The Hot Box   9

→ PDX   13

The Right Tool   17

Tokyo Free Time   25

Tracks   29

Idol   35

Crossing   39

A Reduction of Pearl Tatlin   43

Quince   57

Every Year Like Clockwork   61

Checking Out   65

Traffic   69

An Easy Meal   73

Balance   77

The Wreck of the Conrad Graf   81

Not Georgia   85

Weeds   89

Party   91

Butterflies   95

The Last Days of Comedy   99

Small Measures   113

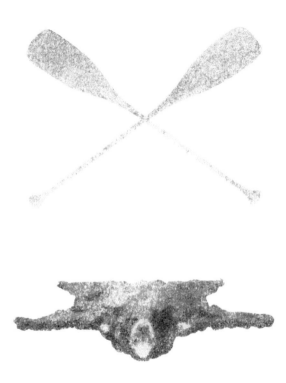

Ursa Minor

Lars Barker-Brown was species non-conforming, a state that had suited him well for some weeks. He hadn't been born a bear or felt as one trapped in something like a man's body. But it was time to explore creative alternatives to being socially adept. His ex-wife's wedding was approaching and Toastmasters had completely failed him.

The idea of bear hit after stumbling across a blog on the Ursine Diet, which consisted of plants, fruits, nuts, insects, honey, salmon, small mammals, and carrion. He was eating most of these already and figured the rest would be easy to add.

It was a start.

Bacterial genome transplantation was a long-term potential way of converting from *homo sapiens* to *ursus arctos horribilis*, but he wasn't made of time. And even Lars could picture being in the crosshairs a couple of autumns down the line. Perhaps the fur and teeth weren't necessary.

The claws, though.

There was something in those.

He recalled Nietzsche's assertion that the mind and soul are completely illusory products of one's physical brain and body. Cursing his decision to be a philosophy major all those years ago, Lars damned the man and turned his attention as usual to the internet. He found an upcoming retreat just outside Jasper devoted to discovering and embracing one's spirit animal. It was a haul from Calgary but those hours would be more affordable than what he'd spent on attempts at speechwriting. In an uncharacteristic fit of self-assurance Lars selected the Second Wind lifetime membership option and punched in his credit card number.

The weekend was something other than he'd hoped, in that the company's set of rituals initially revealed him to be a marmot, or perhaps prairie dog. It was only after hearing a forced growl induced from a false hypnotic state that the group's spiritual coach conceded there might be some measure of bear in Lars.

Maybe a nice cinnamon cub.

It was enough.

The wedding took place at the Gaddis Rowing Club, a stronghold for the Barkers and scene of many a power play. The banquet hall's walls featured crossed oars with many of their names and exploits burned in.

The new husband was Owen Barker-Finch, an assistant coach with the university's crew team and a Mr. British Columbia runner-up from thirty years ago. He had a cleft chin that was losing its depth, and dimples stripped of any charm they might have had during a speed-fueled youth. The steel-grey eyes held strands of rust that radiated from coal circles. The nose was knocked to one side, the left nostril caving slightly. Lars thought of marble busts he'd seen in art classes – yet another waste of time – and imagined this man as the brief victim of an attempted chiseling.

Barker-Finch's ears, ragged cups sprouting tufts, seemed to want to detach from his head. All the same, Lars suspected they picked up on danger. Reasonably alert. Not that listening would matter.

He pegged the guy for a lemur and liked his chances.

At the reception Lars readied himself, conjuring a recent moment in those woods near Jasper that could guide him.

A microphone was passed around the room and people in various states of frivolity and affectation offered commentary. Lars caught only a few words. His name popped up a couple of times, followed by a kind of applause, hand gestures, and some whistles. He dropped his head and focused on his bare feet, seeing only paws and claws.

A work colleague of his ex-wife's finished an anecdote and Lars stood. He raised his arms toward the ceiling and lumbered toward her.

Amid muffled groans and giggles, she handed over the mike with a mock bow.

In moments of self-doubt these past few weeks he'd looked up bear behavior, just in case the spirit left at the wrong moment. He'd learned that when two unacquainted bears come face to face, the rituals of snorting, chomping, huffing, and false charging can serve the same purpose as people's more genteel efforts. Prevent aggression. Possibly forge friendship.

It was nice to know, but he didn't want to send the wrong message.

He raised the mike and locked eyes with the new husband. Standing as high on the balls of his feet as he could muster, Lars issued a low growl that morphed into a sputtering grumble, then a spastic, choking cough. A burst of laughter hit the back of his head and he heard *Gawd, it's the picnic fiasco all over again. Christ on a stick, the little dipshit.* Lars turned toward the offender, snarled, and pulled his lips back to show gums, a couple of which were bleeding. Goddamn oyster shells. He hated himself for breaking the diet on this of all days. A fly landed on his lip and he slapped the crap out of it in an impressive show of reflex. Reeling, but alert enough to try and make this seem entirely intentional, he carried the move through into a vigorous rub of the weedy scruff he'd managed to grow over cheeks and chin these past weeks, adjusted his glasses, wheeled back toward the groom, and reeled off a few good rumbling snorts and huffs. Felt the spirit shoot straight from his eyeballs right to the center of the man's forehead. In a blinding flash of courage and complete abandonment of self he grabbed his crotch, roared, and false-charged the wedding dais.

When he came to, Lars found his ex-father-in-law and various other no-longer relatives standing over him with oars raised. He exhaled heavily, drew his knees into his chest, and regarded the shine off their shoes. How the hell did they get their webbed feet into the damn things?

They stood wrong. Smelled wrong.

Clean.

As blood dripped from nose to carpet, Lars felt a true transformation take him right to where he belonged.

He closed his eyes, gave a nasty possum hiss, and played dead.

A Little More West

They'd nailed a tarnished brass roadrunner above the mantel after Daddy passed. The bird's legs were frozen mid-churn above smoky photos of the kids and their broods; two went face down that morning as Carmen cut through the frames, chasing a spider and snagging a claw on protective cellophane that curled off a snap of the final family trip. A younger Ivy Jo was half out of the shot, hanging a pace from the others, her face and hands washed out by the sun's rays.

She took the picture in hand and stared down the roadrunner.

Everyone had left.

Adabelle wanted to be in all places at all times and was said to suffer from worry that someone in the next room could be preparing a fart and she might miss it.

J.C. was born with just those initials and told by the Army that he needed names for them. He chose the most distinguished ones he could think of: Julius Christian.

And the twins. Elders clear up to Wichita Falls called them angels, saying their voices were God's own melodicas and sure evidence of His great design. Ivy Jo conjured their flapping lips and wondered.

Adjusting the frames, she picked up a whisker Carmen had lost in the heat of the hunt. Twirling it between her fingers, this became a twister. She brought it to her good eye and watched the wild cone engulf Daddy's chair, the busted player piano, and a collection of old thimbles.

Turning idly on her heels while destroying other heirlooms in this way, she caught a grey flash and crossed to the picture window to see what creature the cat was torturing now.

Bastard cabbage kept creeping toward the steps and she told herself to get the man in to hold it back. The beaten porch had taken an iron hue since supper and the clouds were tall and heading green. As a girl, she'd been told this happened when the billows sucked up grasshoppers and frogs. They kicked in their fury at big blocks of ice and sent hail hauling toward the crops. These days, the field was home only to the Dodge. The rusted heap sat stupid in the yard growing weeds, a reminder to check her blood pressure.

Ivy Jo pulled the whisker through her fingers, trying to straighten it out. At the first thunderclap, she stuck it between her teeth and brushed off her sleeves.

"Car-*men*! Carmen Davis, you get up here, boy!"

The clouds sat high over a sprawling plate of charred potential that drew her eye to the distant line over which so many had disappeared. *Not today, not ever*, she thought, as the cat slunk under the house.

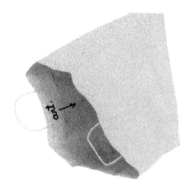

The Hot Box

Every act on No-Talent Night at Al's Bar lives up to expectations.

This time it started with Paint Box, a twee duo from Fullerton who played Joy Division covers on ukulele and zither. They'd planned for three songs but got kicked after one and change and apologized for any bother they might have caused.

It had been a scorcher and the bar offered no relief, even though by design it properly shut out the sun. No fans, no air conditioning, and the place reeked of leaky skin, dirty bedclothes, and sunscreen.

There was a large oilcloth stretched behind the stage from one end to the other. This read Catolitica Converter in thick black strokes of a paintbrush, the Cs crossed out with Xs and a faint Perverter scrawled underneath in crayon. The large drum kit already in place suggested this was the night's one legit band waiting off-stage to play a proper set once the talentless were done.

After Paint Box got ousted, Rhythm Box (no relation) took the stage. No instruments. Just a grocery bag and three people dressed as lifeguards. One bikini and two trunks. The bikini would pull some product out of the bag and one of the trunks would apply it to the other trunk. Grape jelly, baked beans, yogurt. With each new item, the crowd – 16 people, not bad – would belch admiring noises. A few started shouting out items they wanted to see get used. "Cajun seasoning!" "Molasses!" "Red dye #2!" The trunks, anticipating this, said in a stereo monotone, "We don't do requests."

A few started throwing their plastic beer cups at the lifeguard trio.

9

Only one managed to connect, and the tosser shouted, "I want cheese! You can't leave without doing cheese!"

As if by some kind of crap magic, the last item produced was a tub of cream cheese. The good kind. The tosser screamed with delight. "You fuckers! You *beautiful* fuckers!" He tore off his t-shirt, threw it at a sulking Paint Box, and jumped onto the stage, grabbing his prize from the bikini. He struggled to break the seal, his hands being wet with beer and sweat, but finally managed and took deep fingerfuls of the white whip, smearing it in his armpits, across his chest, a little behind the ears, and some for a moustache. He raised his arms in victory and made for the trunks, as if to demolish them with a violently grateful hug. In their rush to escape, they slipped on all the dripped foodstuffs and fell to the floor. The tosser, with outstretched arms and legs, dove on top.

Seeing this flying X land on most of what had to be considered a highly successful talentless trio, the audience stormed the stage and broke into a spasm of slides and spills.

From the wings, the lead singer of Catolitica Converter told the rest of the band that they couldn't and shouldn't go on.

It's good to know when it's not your night.

→ PDX

Watch again.

Carefully this time.

Take cab along straight and narrow.

Travel long way around from St. Joan's head to golden horse's ass.

Stare into K-9 cop's mirrored lenses.

Look at watch.

Look at cyclist.

Listen to Ethiopian maybe Somali maybe Eritrean music coming from stereo.

Create song in head using only memorable line from that morning's presidential briefing.

Have third personality use psycho persuasive power to will driver to stay in best possible lane.

Check current lottery jackpot amount on billboard.

Calculate how much earned per minute from time of lottery win to predicted end of life.

Promise self some beer at airport if cab passes light rail train before 205 turnoff.

Play Admiral Halsey song in head.

Pinch skin hard on back of hand for doing that Admiral Halsey thing.

Rank cars by popularity.

Give top prize for week to Honda Fit.

Consider whether name was chosen for fitness or fitfulness.

Look at watch.

Look at cow on truck's milk tanks.

Try to calculate amount of milk generated on planet to date.

Have second personality use psycho persuasive power to will planet to keep spinning.

Imagine size of container to hold all fingernail and toenail clippings for which personally responsible.

Suck stomach in.

Straighten shirt cuffs.

Remember last time flew to Midwest.

Wonder why there's no Mideast.

Have fourth personality use psycho persuasive power to compel all responsible parties to back away from must-haves.

Meet eyes of driver in rearview mirror.

Open notebook with apparent intent.

Focus all energy on IKEA sign.

Make note in book: International airport – IKEA, IHOP, Panda Express.

Feel feet itch.

Look at watch.

Use psycho persuasive power to will time to slow up.

Use psycho persuasive power to will time to slow up.

Try pleading with all personalities to make time slow up.

Ask driver to be let out next to horse sculptures.

Tell driver to keep suitcase.

Count to 10.

Look at watch.

Count down from 5.

Laugh too loudly.

The Right Tool

Gyp woke up, which he took as a sign.

Earlier, he nailed one hand to the floor in a fit of manufactured despair and misappropriated identity, realizing a few seconds and screams later that he'd be unable to complete the self-crucifixion gag so long as where he held the hammer was also where the second nail needed to go. He choked down a scream and tried to reverse the process.

The shame of it all was that if someone walked through the door, they'd have seen a squirming snakelike "C" trying to detach from the floor, not the humanlike "T" he envisioned, face up and beatific in his white jumpsuit. He stopped struggling and lay flat on his back. Closing his eyes, he concentrated on the pinch between nail head and floor, screamed once more, then used his meditation teacher's technique for shifting to another time and place.

Transformed by this trip, Gyp rolled onto his side and grabbed one of the many pens scattered across the floor. He scrawled on his wrist *try this one – swinging jesus southpaw giant*, just where the blood trailed away from the pinned palm.

Satisfied, he went ahead and passed out.

The studio smelled of varnish and waste. Paintings gathered dust and bugs. Years of sloppy encaustic work left the floor splattered with beeswax, making a lumpy matte carpet over low-grade plywood. Someone practiced cello above. A musical saw cut through from below.

The light was good. So was the heater. Too good. Couldn't keep it on long for fear of melting the more fragile pieces.

All of this had been fine, just fine.

But with only a few days to go, Gyp spent more time staring at the two pieces he'd made for the Home Remedies group show at NINEONE1 Cooperative Arts than working on the required third piece.

Rejection was the norm of late.

He'd turned his back on painting to try mixed media. Found objects repurposed. Bought objects de-purposed. He made lists of names for potential works and had a vague idea that everything he created could be viewed as a household tool.

For the right household.

He even concocted stories surrounding each piece. One involved a person with dissociative identity disorder trying to eliminate unwanted personalities by using a device made specifically to that end. Another spun around a man who couldn't keep secrets and thus spoke them into a crude vessel he'd fashioned and stoppered, but which had begun to split from the strain.

It all became too ethereal, and Gyp felt himself floating away.

A nail and a hammer grounded him.

As he regained consciousness, the thought occurred to him that maybe the studio wasn't fine. It felt toxic lately. Even worse, stagnant. Maybe he needed to catch a spark through a change of scenery. Gyp considered the hammer still clutched in his good hand and the idea hit: he would plant the two finished pieces at the local hardware store and see what reaction they got. In the process, he might figure out what to do for a third.

He jammed the hammer claw between the nail head and fleshy mess of his palm and yelled as loud as he could, hoping to drown out the pain he was sure would come. He hadn't counted on doing such a good job of securing himself to the floor, and it took several efforts to achieve detachment.

Blood pooled. The cello droned.

With any good plan you need accomplices, and his were a pair of baby monitors he picked up some years before with a view to catching his roommate talking by phone on the sly with Gyp's then-girlfriend. The ploy was successful and thus at least one cause of anxiety was eliminated, although coming up with the rent on his own since the breakup had been tricky. He trusted these plastic partners and planned to use them to hear reactions to his pieces in the hardware store while pretending to peruse stock.

Gyp undid the jumpsuit with his good hand, tucked the receiving monitor into his underwear, then zipped back up. He shoved the transmitter and art pieces into the sad-eyed sloth bookbag he'd found outside an elementary school. The excitement of the store idea momentarily erased all pain, and he only then thought to wrap his bad hand with an oily rag before striking out.

Trailing drops of blood for several blocks, Gyp pushed through the front door of the store, tripping a bell and then himself as the doormat flipped up and sent him reeling toward a rack of discounted shovels. A teen in a grease-streaked shop apron briefly raised her eyes from the checkout station, then returned to using the edge of the counter to tear paper into small strips to the beat of dance music that squeaked from an emergency crank radio. Gyp picked up a shovel and turned it over in his hands, feigning interest and hoping to deflect attention from the noisy entrance. Finding that nobody was noticing at all, however, began to aggravate him. He planted the blade in an adjacent stack of bagged compost.

Gyp paced a few aisles, determining which section of the store deserved to show off his particular brand of tools and scanning for potentially complementary or ironic pairings with his pieces. He chose a shelf displaying megaphones and slid the transmitting baby monitor behind them. Realizing he needed to give his pieces some legitimacy as store items, Gyp stole a marker and some labels, on which he wrote down the tools' names and prices: Voices Degenerator: $314.159265. Secrets Retainer: $411. He affixed them to the shelf. Then, on the off-chance that someone who appreciated art would recognize his work for what it truly was, he reached into the backpack and pulled out a couple of business cards. These read GYP ROSEN on one side and TOURIST on the other. Placing them a little behind each of the pieces, he wandered off, happy to let the monitors do their work.

The process took a good while, and by then Gyp was dripping a fair amount of blood. He cinched the rag a bit tighter, wiped his hands on the front of the jumpsuit, and used his foot to hide the pool collecting on the floor. He started reading product labels just loud enough to attract Big Walt, the store's owner, who looked him up and down before asking, "Do you need help?"

Gyp's response was snuffed by a great plaid donkey of a man who'd been shadowing Walt through the store and now patted his shoulder to ask, "What the hell's this Voices Generator?"

Walt looked at the confused mess of materials the man held, excused himself from Gyp and said, "Speak English, Norm."

Gyp took his advantage.

"Yeah, that can't be right. I mean, it would make sense if it was a Voices *De*generator, but a Voices Generator would be weird."

"Our buyer knows what he's doing," said Walt. "If people want generators, that's what we sell them."

Gyp leaned over and gave the tool his professional eye, saying, "This is definitely a Voices Degenerator. Better stores have them. I'm not surprised you've got this in stock."

Norm considered this and asked, "What do you use them for? It just looks like a fancy hand mirror with a junky piece of plywood instead of glass. The handle's all cut up."

"Pretty sure it's for helping schizophrenics get rid of their extra personalities," said Gyp.

"Well, hell, I have no idea why that would be here," said Walt. "Outside old Norm here, we don't usually get fruitcakes in until just before Christmas."

Warming to his role, Gyp asked, "If you've got Voices Degenerators, you probably also have Secrets Retainers. Where do you keep those?"

Walt stared at a point between Gyp's eyes and said, "I don't think I got that right. What kind of containers?"

"Well, do you have bullhorns? Secrets Retainers are usually in the same area."

"If you mean megaphones, then yes." Walt cupped his hands around his mouth and shouted across the store, "Angie, do we have any Secrets Retainers over by the Finex Megasonics?" He winked at Norm and chuckled. It took a minute for the reply.

"We've just got one left."

The voice simultaneously shot across the ceiling and exited Gyp's crotch as a tinny echo. Walt turned and stared at him. Sliding one boot ahead of the other, he planted himself firmly in the middle of the aisle.

"Why is my wife's voice coming out of your pants?"

Norm offered, "If you're hearing double, Walt, maybe you should use this degenerator thing to help fix that."

Walt gave Norm a long, hard stare. Gyp used the distraction to pivot and turn off the speaker through the suit's fabric. As he did, he spotted a boy in a soccer uniform who'd skipped into the aisle from the opposite end, honking through a kazoo.

And that was it. His moment of clarity. The third piece. A Prodigy Protector. As Walt explained to Norm the difference between generators and degenerates, Gyp, growing fainter, imagined this new tool and the story surrounding it.

Turning back toward Walt, he said, "I think I need some latex gloves, ready-mix cement, and duct tape."

"You think?" asked Walt. "What's your project?"

"Well, I've got a 13-year-old in mind," Gyp mused, drifting into a reverie as he became more lightheaded and his body grew weaker.

Walt took a closer look at the man before him; only then did he see the blood and the strange message written on his wrist. Taking in the child's backpack, and noting the glazed look in Gyp's eyes, Walt's face turned to borscht.

"I don't believe we can help you," he said, fingering the box cutter attached to his belt.

Gyp wobbled. Nothing looked right but it all felt perfect. He looked up at a flickering fluorescent lamp and his bad hand's stigma seemed to buzz with energy. He lifted his arm toward the light, and the rag fell off.

Walt made a move toward him, but Gyp managed to edge out of the way. He snatched the Voices Degenerator from Norm's hand, then stumbled through the store shouting into it, "He is Rosen! He is Rosen!"

Overweight and up in years, Walt had trouble keeping pace but managed to get in a tackle just as Gyp reached the Secrets Retainer and grabbed for it. The two men went down in a heap, with the artist's tools breaking to bits beneath them.

As they waited for the police, Walt tallied the damage and determined that, whatever Gyp might be, he owed him $725.159265 in lost goods plus untold additional medical expenses.

Gyp smiled, pleased to have sold his pieces. In the moment before it all went black, he considered changing the back of his business card to read PARTICIPANT.

It was enough.

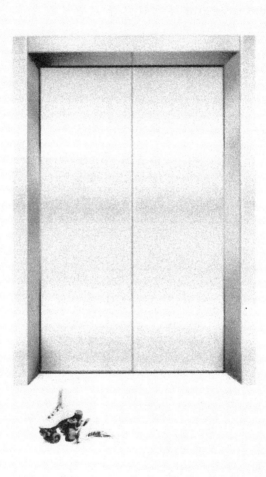

Tokyo Free Time

There's a stretch of Komazawa Dori the yakimo vendors avoid. It starts near the train station, where the free-timers hand out facial tissue packets advertising mobile phone deals, and ends several blocks away close to the shrine. Raw yakimo are cheap at the station's market, and incense escaping the shrine can mask the smell of these sweet potatoes roasting over wood fires burning in the vendors' truck beds. The threat of an explosion lurks but the yakimo are always worth it.

The vendors and their trucks mostly stick to the interior streets. Just residents. Little competition.

A fog of pink lanterns hovers over the plaza that fronts the station. The Setsubun festival that always celebrates spring much too early has happened already, with cries of *Oni wa soto! Fuku wa uchi!* (Demons out! Luck in!) having died in the streets weeks earlier. It's cold season and the free-timers are running out of tissue packets. Some slow down the handouts, stretching the hours toward what could pass for real work. The ones dressed for later fun practically toss them into the crowd. Nothing moves quickly enough for them.

A soothing recorded voice announces the arrival of a train and they all gear up for another stream of people. A few free-timers move closer to the exit, thanking the commuters for taking the free gift before it's even handed over. A reeling salaryman, face blown red with drink, crashes through a turnstile and knocks a hand clutching tissues, sending packets flying. The free-timer apologizes a bit too loudly for the commuter's blunder and the man turns toward her, taken aback.

The moment drains some of the blood from his face, almost erasing the deep flush below his eyes. He doesn't know whether to offer an apology in kind or let her continue to express regret for her role in his mistake. He drops his eyes to her shoes. These are massive platforms plastered with peeling stickers of both The Bathing Ape and an aging American singer who's enjoying renewed popularity this year thanks to a TV ad for an over-the-counter gastrointestinal relief tablet. Seeing the free-timer's feet so high above the ground reminds him of a time when he floated through the old neighborhood, roller-skating alongside his dog. Those weren't great years either, but thinking of skimming just a little above the pavement, toward the train tracks and along the levee, makes his lip twitch toward a smile.

The other commuters have moved past him. It seems time has, too. He picks up the one tissue package not yet gathered by the free-timer, who with each shout makes clear there is no real apology behind this at all. The commuter raises the package to his forehead, bows slightly toward her, conjures one last image of the dog, turns toward the plaza, and steps into the street.

When the company publishes his obituary a few days later, there is no mention of how he died. How a yakimo vendor who'd been uncharacteristically driving near the station struck him down. Instead, it tells of years of commitment, focus, and consistency. Of the time he gave that speech. Of the joke he told all the new interns.

The vendor sends a basket of perfect yakimo, which the head of HR places on an altar near the elevator. Everyone takes out a tissue when they stand near it, for the first couple of days.

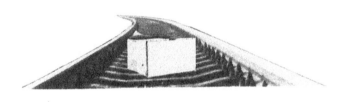

Tracks

— Did I ever tell you about the time I didn't die?

We lived in Chatsworth in the early 70s. Tract housing. Everything in that corner of the valley was just getting built up. You'd still see wolves.

I did once, anyway.

The Family did its thing a few years before. Manson had been put away, and us kids heard what Spahn Ranch was; we thought it sounded like a badass Western theme park. It was there, up in the Santa Susana Mountains, and we wanted to see it. Once or twice a week after school – about 4th grade, I guess – we'd start up that way but only get as far as the tracks. A bend around some rocks let us stay hidden from the trains, and we'd hang out for a couple of hours, watching them trail through, looking down at our neighborhood in the distance through the open freight cars that split us from it.

The mother sat up and shook her head.

— Can you imagine what it's like to stab someone?

The father considered his reflection in the knife for a few seconds.

— Sure, we've all pulled a few weeds.

He continued.

— I don't remember who got the bright idea, but one day we decided it'd be more interesting if we lay down on the tracks while waiting for a train. We picked the one that showed up at the same time every afternoon, a little more than an hour after school. After watching it for a few days, we tested whether it would pass over us OK by putting a cardboard box on the tracks with a couple of big rocks inside to hold it down. It worked. The train sped right over, driver didn't even seem to care about the box, certainly didn't slow down any, and the cardboard flapped only a little bit at the end of it all.

We'd seen a train try to come to a quick stop once before, but it didn't seem to be the kind of thing that happened too fast. That was good enough for us. We went back the next day and lay down at that bend, feet to shoulders, four boys long.

I only remember Roger's name now. Don't know why.

We kept our heads up so we could look at the train as it came at us. When it did, I couldn't spot anyone in the engine car, but someone definitely saw us because the horn went off. I dropped my head back and looked straight at the sky. Got ready. In a few seconds, it was every sound you could imagine – the end of the world. Metal on metal, rattling slats, clanging couplings, god knows what else, and the horn blew through it all. I stared into the undercarriages, or whatever they call them.

The sun came through with every gap between cars, and the switches from dark to light above us clicked along for what seemed forever. I wanted to tilt my head forward to see the friends at my feet but my whole body felt glued to the wooden ties. The squealing wheels got worse, but the horn started to fade.

Sounded like a lonely old dog stuck inside some house way down the street.

The kid with his feet on my shoulders sometimes twitched, but otherwise we were locked in place. And the sun kept sweeping across us through the couplings. Sometimes I'd see something carved into the belly of a car. Or maybe it was some image the factory stamped in. Felt like a message, one way or another. I started to wonder if our cardboard box had just got lucky. Every now and then I'd see a piece of chain hanging down, and it occurred to me that one of these could end us.

A little bit of wind would catch and lift my shirt sometimes, filling it like a sail then letting go.

The gaps of light started to feel longer as the roar began to die. I was able to raise my head a bit and saw that the two kids past my feet had crossed their arms over their chests. The one at the end of our link stared out the side, past the wheels and down the hill. I tried that too, but it was all stuff I'd seen before. Although I guess the wheels cutting in front of my eyes did a little something different for the view.

The boy at my shoulders started to kick now, and I realized that what I thought was all horn actually included a real weird scream. Like if someone slugged you in the throat and you tried to yell for help while grabbing for air. The kid – this was no Roger – wanted out.

We hadn't exactly planned our escape, and I felt locked in place. Hadn't noticed it before, but now one of the ties really started to dig into my back, and my hands clutched gravel. The horn stopped, seeming to just give up, and the ride felt over. I saw the name of the wheel company etched into the metal as it rolled past and decided everything was moving slow enough to cut out.

The twitcher's feet clipped my ears. I turned to see him kicking dust, his head dipping over the edge of the slope as he hit it back to our neighborhood. I went next, and we all peeled off that way one after the other, slipping between the wheels.

If the driver ever saw us, I don't know. Don't remember hearing anything particularly human at any point, including that boy's noise.

Everyone should do this. I still play it all out in my head whenever I want.

The mother knocked her shoulder hard into the father's.

— Tell him the other story.

— I don't like that one anymore.

— But it's funny.

The father dragged his knife through mashed potatoes, made a grid, dropped a couple of pieces of corn in different squares, and turned to the son.

— Hate's a shameful thing, boy.

He turned the knife in his hand, used the handle to push the kernels of corn into the potatoes, and gave the son his news.

— By the way, I'm having my heart replaced.

— Your *heart*?

The father looked up, startled, as though he'd just heard the information for the first time.

— No. Not heart. The other one. Knee. Although you never know what they're really doing once you're under. You're out for the whole thing. They might actually *put* a heart in down there. Or a rubber duck. You don't know. They tell you everything went great, show you an X-ray, and because they just about typed your name right on the thing, you're supposed to believe that's a picture of some part of you.

The son shook his head and stuck his thumb into the torn foam of the booth's seat.

— I don't see the problem.

— There is no problem.

The mother leaned forward and whispered to the son, as if there were spies everywhere.

— Your dad doesn't like hospitals because of what happened to his dad there.

The son couldn't remember this story of his father's and that perked him up.

— He got hit by a car and died instantly.

The mother hacked up a smoker's cackle.

— Everybody always says the man died in childbirth. He got smacked running outside blindly into the ER turnaround, shouting about your dad being born. It was a Ford Falcon.

The father put the knife on the table and gave it a spin.

— Corvair. And it wasn't so much a blind situation.

He entered a reverie, fixing his gaze on a gouge in the tabletop.

— Forgot that Roger moved away a couple of months after the train. Didn't talk much those last weeks. Everybody sees things different, I guess.

The waitress asked if she could interest anyone in a slice of pie.

Nobody was interested, so she left the bill.

The father paid what he owed and settled back.

Idol

There's a baby out there with eyes covered in crystalline onyx scales. But no ears. It doesn't know about death yet and has no thought of loss.

The kid scoops up shiny objects with long basket hands formed from weaves that spring from its middle fingers and already are unraveling. Most of its face is a vacuum mouth that sucks everything from these catchalls directly into its stomach, a mill powered by smoke that siphons through a small pinprick in the top of its head.

The child grinds and excretes ideas through the thousand other holes that comprise its body, and these turn into paper bills that burst into flame and make more smoke. It sleeps in the ashes, which keep it warm and grey. The baby has a hundred big toes with which to try to plug the holes, but that's well short and its body makes an imploding bellows wheeze.

It has a crimson, scabrous, oily tail that starts from between the legs but coils tightly around the neck. When sensing a need to protect, this spins off in a long spiral that stabs blindly into the air. If it happens to hit something, the end of the tail – a dull, overused point – makes a notch at the back of the head. There are a few deep grooves there already.

Our baby only ever says one word – *want* – but everyone hears this as train wheels screeching mercilessly along rusted rail. The sound travels for miles before fading into muted laughter.

It rocks back and forth in the ashes, and when its body sneezes in reaction, the cloud is large and dense enough to block out the town's light.

For this and other less definable reasons, people keep bringing it more shiny objects that it can never properly see.

Crossing

The whole thing had been on fire once.

A few swore to this. Saw it at night some way off the highway. One described it as a tray of flame that hung steady in the air and that's how you knew exactly what was burning. They'd taken a few things that day, though, and had more than one vision.

But you could just tell something was coming.

Generations of strain weakened the long twists of rope. Sharp bristles spun from knots, and fraying lengths fell a few feet to punctuate the ends of tired slats. A feather might catch and linger in one of the fibrous knuckles; others were purposely stabbed with toothpicks and bobby pins, breaking the tension just a little. Splatters of teenage spit and piss that didn't make it into the creek – a completely dry rock bed at this time of year – speckled the wood and died in the cracks. The rocky end of the bridge was secured with rusted railway spikes. The other side lashed to two sycamores that blazed in October and shimmered in spring.

It all worked well enough until Pudge Crawford busted a slat with her foot, split another with her ass and knocked her chin on yet one more piece of wood. Bit off her tongue mid-scream as she dropped toward the bed.

They served ham sandwiches at the council meeting and the mayor trotted out his floating witch joke. Someone asked if it wasn't true that there hadn't been a fire running the bridge there a while back, and a number shook their heads.

You just knew that there was something at work out there.

The vote went 6-1 in favor of preservation, and the creek swelled with rain like you wouldn't believe.

A Reduction of Pearl Tatlin

She liked counting and dividing. Couldn't read a book without focusing on the characters in each word and determining whether they were an odd or even number. In her head, she deleted all odd words, creating new phrases comprised only of even ones. Pearl found this all read much better and created a more meaningful message. One that she'd managed to intercept from her mind. The opening sentence to David Copperfield was reduced to *turn to be hero of my or that will be held by must*. Yes. That was more like it. And Melville got to the point right out of the gate. *Call me*.

She didn't need to read between the lines. Just cut them down. Perfection would be a book in which all the sentences were made up of odd-numbered characters. Then everything could be deleted.

There was genius in empty space and the art of no line being drawn at all.

Pearl sensed that she shouldn't really exist and made plans to disappear. Not blend in or be unnoticed. Simply fade away. Her impact while stuck here should be less than minimal. She would have no footprint, no sense of having been. She'd taken to the idea two years earlier. Her parents were outgoing sorts, which really put her off. Themed parties and mosquito-infested luaus in summer and brandied nog fests in winter. The air at these events hung thick with scented candles and bad jokes, and she clung to the wall. Even though she didn't want to be, as it were, Pearl liked to hear. To absorb the effluent that passed for conversation. She gathered certain words and phrases from the crowd and let them roam around her head, where they dissolved. She considered her ideas and beliefs to be hers and hers alone, although Pearl's mom always seemed to sense her deepest reveries. She'd blow Pearl a kiss at such times, put her index fingers to her eyes, wiggle them at her daughter, and cry out, *Cockeyed*!

Sometimes Pearl wiggled back.

The family had a dog that Pearl had taken to calling Dr. Ellen F. Cranwick, a rat terrier with a 500-word vocabulary. At least, this is what Pearl expected from the breed, based on her readings. The trick was to find out how many words they both knew. If Dr. C threw out something she heard as *pedantic*, there might be an issue. Pearl only knew the word phonetically and wanted to keep it that way. She understood *bathetic*, though, and suspected most dogs didn't. Not even the good doctor. They conducted language class each afternoon together, sitting perfectly still on the couch comparing words. Depending on the day, Dr. C instead might be focusing more on the cracker shrapnel that had worked its way between the cushions. Or maybe she was contemplating what it meant to be named after a rat and the intellectual implications that held. But the two of them seemed to be on the same plane, conjuring words. Up to 500.

Which is likely more than you need.

Progress was slow, and Pearl started to keep a kind of score. Incentive for them both. On one occasion, the good doctor suddenly snapped with purpose at an unseen unwanted on her flank, snarfing and shnorking.

Snarf and shnork are weak efforts, thought Pearl. *Full point to me.*

Dr. C wheezed, in seeming agreement.

The hours were long and her mom, on a good day, sometimes remembered to ask her to go outside. Pearl felt exposed. Her dad called her over to the pool too often, trying to get her to jump into the damn thing. After all, he'd put it in for her. Whether she liked it or not. And who the hell wouldn't want a pool? Think of the boys. And if not the boys, think of the girls.

Pearl's mom had her own Dr. C somewhere out there that Pearl had never met. Her dad would say his wife was a real piece of work, adding, *She's funny hmmm, not funny ahhh. You know?* Told people who met her for the first time that she was a fabulous babe who'd gone to Yale for a bit. Just to provide some context. Lay the groundwork.

Her mom did the cockeyed thing with her fingers and eyes at such times. Or some other favorite hilarity.

There was a photo in one of the coffee table books of an armless nude sculpture referred to as a masterwork, and Pearl wondered if her mom was cut from the same jib. That's how you're supposed to use that set of words, she was fairly sure. Her mom might even be a jib and a half. She liked the scent of her jib. On one rare occasion, her mom drove to school to retrieve Pearl, calling across the passenger seat, *There's too much to do! Let's hit it, Lord Snowden!* This was remarkable enough that the kids who heard couldn't make much out of it, so at least the name didn't stick.

She started to skip classes.

Pearl had one friend and one enemy. The friend was Pilar Nawaz, the enemy Sookie Tarkanian. And they all knew each other pretty well and got along nicely. As enemies went, in fact, Sookie was a fair disappointment. Pearl wanted mutual hate to be at play but there wasn't much there. So she merely assigned Sookie the role of enemy in her head and let that be that.

Pilar's case was about the same.

They rarely came to the house and she returned the favor by generally staying away from theirs. As Pearl played hooky more and more, Pilar joked that she was starting to forget what her friend looked like.

This made Pearl beam.

At school, it hadn't been terribly difficult for her to just about disappear. When she did show up for class the teachers didn't call on her. They seemed to properly recognize that there was no need to bother her with these matters. And when she wasn't there they figured that was about right and didn't contact her parents. Pearl liked her mom's Gogol book, and the way the words reduced in her mind, but got stuck with an English literature class. Austen had nothing for her. And the Brontes were fully loaded. Not enough words came up odd, so the stories stayed bloated.

In the evenings, Pearl collapsed on the living room floor and tried to use telepathy to will Dr. C to do certain things. If the good doctor simply raised her head, despite no apparent noise, Pearl would chalk this up to her unseen powers. But often it would turn out that Dr. C had reasonable enough hearing to pick up on a car door closing in the driveway. Or some paper shifting along the desk in the next room. Pearl once tried to compel her to run to the entertainment center, touch it with her nose, then run back to the sofa. The good doctor merely lifted her head and set it back down again.

Pearl claimed a minor victory.

She decided that the best way to disappear was to make the act seem super normal. Try not to have too much of an impact on the world. For starters, she stopped eating and drinking a number of things. They mostly were bad for you anyway, and it surely hurts to be eaten and drunk. *And cows are lovely and goats are lovely*, she'd muse. *I don't want to deal with them but also don't want them to suffer just because I like delicious burgers and tasty cheese and silky yogurt.*

Dr. C always seemed compelled to trot in when Pearl entered such a reverie – a word they both knew.

Her parents, classmates, and teachers seemed only a little affected by her new actions and inactions. And not to the point where they were getting noisy about it. So she kept it up. Added to the subtractive mix, even. Pearl stayed away from anything that could be recycled. Things should just evaporate. She took to wearing only a couple sets of pants and shirts.

Linen. Matched the sea grass wallpaper in the living room.

If there was one thing her dad knew, it was that even if you shouldn't have been born, you're here now so have fun with it. He didn't quite put it that way, instead saying, *You gotta do your thing, dog,* which didn't support his case. Unlike Pearl, he made himself a presence. He'd drop his pants at a party if it seemed that might be required. And he never felt it wasn't. No challenge was refused. He would tell everyone he had a record of 300-0 when it came to such stuff and had consumed just about everything out there: animal, vegetable, mineral, insectoidal, rubberesque, plasticate, marbled, and scaldy. Pearl once caught him in conversation with the mirrored medicine cabinet, saying, *Tatlin, you've got it*.

One time a raw chicken wing intended for the grill fell off a platter and onto the patio. It was a pretty good day for Pearl's mom, who thought to dare him to put the capsized flesh in the path of some ants and chomp any that wound up on the meat. But none did. No matter how much he readjusted it to be in their way. Pearl watched from her window upstairs as he ate the wing anyway, and knew he'd chalk it up as a minor victory.

It wasn't the first time they'd seen a situation like this at the ER, which she could tell was disappointing for him. Pearl weighed herself a few times on a scale outside his hospital room while her mom joked with the doctor about evolution and demonstrated a dance she called The Piss-Ant.

Only a couple of years ago, Pearl would have spent hours drawing riotous landscapes and quirky portraits. She'd start by sprawling face down on her bedroom floor, attacking a huge pad of newsprint with pastel sticks, carving out images that erupted just inches from her eyes. But now she shunned such materials. They were just an excuse to create more and more clutter. Same went for paint and canvases. Her art became about rearranging things that already existed. Interlacing twigs. Relocating rocks. Moving a lamp. Leaving streaks in the carpet by dragging her fingers through it, later seeing them get wiped away by the vacuum cleaner or her mom, on a good day, making strange movements over the spot that she insisted were exercises. Pearl's favorite art to look at was abstract, but not the kind in museums. More along the lines of her dad's filthy handprints on the monogrammed towels, knowing the dirt would get washed away.

She figured it was OK to hang off a wall but nothing should be in a frame.

In the days before her 13th birthday, Pearl started giving things away. She took clothes to the secondhand shop and donated the $12 earned to a man reclining on a backpack, mostly so he could feed the wordless dog beside him. She delivered both her telescope and microscope to Sookie's housekeeper, whom she'd only met once but who clearly liked to see through things. Pearl kept her dictionary, to further the study of shared vocabulary with Dr. C, but snuck her thesaurus onto a shelf in the school.

She kept her tennis socks, which intrigued her, but got rid of the shoes. The game was all grunts and pop-de-pops, and you could get that just about anywhere else in life.

And she kept her terrarium as a model for how things could be.

Dr. C was seemingly oblivious to all these efforts. Pearl sometimes reached over to pet the good doctor before catching herself in time. *No need to create a disruption just because I want something nice*, she thought. Often, Dr. C seemed properly out of it. Pearl would wonder if she was having a conversation in her dreams with some creature that understood her perfectly.

Or at worst maybe a parallel Pearl.

She was down to eating vegetables, or often just vegetable. Perhaps a radish or stalk of celery. Pearl had read about humane ways of slaughtering cows and pigs and the idea made her shudder. Seemed so sneaky. There should be a last few moments of proper fear. She remembered hearing about a pig that escaped moments before it was to be killed and went barreling down a road's culvert, ultimately being captured but spared. Rewarded for its effort and bravery. Maybe that's all we wanted out of animals in our hold. If they just told us they didn't want to be eaten, perhaps we'd think about it.

Pearl looked at the carrot in her hand and swore she heard it scream.

Water was her favorite. Except to swim in, of course. She drank it daily in real quantity. On her mom's good days, she would tell Pearl it was dangerous to down as much liquid as she did because it could wash out certain vital nutrients, and maybe it would be better if she got more sun on her skin instead of worrying about the possible toxins inside her.

It's too soon for all this, she'd say. *Give it time.*

Sookie periodically came by with homework since Pearl had stayed away from school for a couple of weeks, often hiding out in the basement considering which of her parents' things she could give away. *Finally, she's become a proper enemy*, thought Pearl, as her schoolmate was doing little more than adding material to the pile. On one occasion she stood in the front hall letting the doorbell ring, even though Sookie clearly had spotted her through the side window. Pearl took this chance to practice making herself invisible, staying perfectly still and not letting even one strand of hair move. Sookie cemented her reputation as an enemy by trying the door, finding it unlocked, and stepping inside. *I don't know if you're getting weird or stupid*, she said, handing over sheets of work to be tackled and adding that the art teacher wanted a small portfolio of still life charcoal drawings by the end of the week. She warned that if Pearl didn't do that she'd be left out of the end-of-term wax casting project. The idea here was to make representations of the school mascot for display on a folding table at the entrance to the multipurpose room. But Pearl determined that there were only so many ways you could fashion sculptures of cobras, and most no doubt would wind up looking like coiled crap. Many of them purposely so.

Pearl decided she could just compose a song about snakes and wax and play it in her head during the unveiling of the projects.

I just saw you blink, said Sookie. *You lose.*

Some days later, Pearl took a Polaroid of her dad heating soup on the stove, still in the can. He turned toward the sound of the image spitting out, at which point the can's label caught fire. Pearl snapped another shot and explained, *It's for art*, to which he replied, *Yes it is*. She drew a dozen nearly identical charcoal versions of the photo, then signed and backdated them. Pearl arranged the drawings on her bed in a grid, took a shot of the collection, and burned the originals in her garbage can. She block-printed STILL LIFES: TATLIN in marker on the back of this new photo but decided not to turn it in to the teacher, sliding it under her pillow instead. After a minute, she realized her big mistake and pulled it out again, blacking out the odd-numbered words and leaving just TATLIN.

This reduction disturbed her.

Birthday number 13 was in a week. 2/2/2002. Pearl pictured the date in her head and loved the way it looked. All the 2s were kept apart and the zeroes were friendly. Not to mention that

$2 + 2 + 2 + 0 + 0 + 2 = 8 =$ infinity standing up. This was highly auspicious – a word Dr. C seemed to have tossed out recently.

There would be a collection of local relatives and as many friends as Pearl would like to invite. She wouldn't like to invite anyone, actually, but agreed to let Pilar and Sookie know about the party. It was a good day for her mom, who asked what she'd want served for the birthday dinner. Pearl replied, *Just a few reductions, please.* Manners were the one excess she appreciated. Her mom folded her arms and stuck her neck forward slightly. *You mean soup?* Pearl considered this. *Whatever boils down nicely. Not too many ingredients. And nothing from or by animals. Please.*

This would be a proper themed party, even if she was the only one who understood it.

There are days that seem to flail madly, spectacularly, through the time they occupy. Offering chances, or simply mesmerizing. But on Pearl's day there were no clouds, no leaves on the trees, and an invisible cold slicked the windows.

In all the subdued excitement of preparing for the party, nobody remembered to slide the patio door open for Dr. C to do her business, even though she'd thrown her words at them. So, the good doctor went on the porcelain umbrella stand in the entry. This featured a scene of a small rural village, presumably Chinese, that had been caught in a stylized rainstorm, so the pool of liquid that now formed at the base wasn't terribly out of context. Pearl watched Dr. C finish and click a short couple of steps along the tiled floor to the living room carpet. The good doctor sank her claws into it and scratched with vigor, seemingly confident that she was hiding the recent business behind her. She trotted off, no need to look back.

Pearl propped up against a ceramic elephant that was just big and small enough to earn a place in the living room, and from which she could see her mom fixating on the refrigerator. One of the worst offenders in the house. A monument to spoilage, much of which was on its door. Magnets locked everything in place. A wallet-sized 1996 calendar from the insurance agent. A takeout menu for the Indian place they'd walked into once. Some fitness center's class schedule. And all the damn drawings and photos.

Her stomach growled.

Pearl watched her mom, who never looked at any of that garbage, peel an object from the fridge. Weird. From the shape of it and the way the corners curled, this had to be the ancient stupid horse sketch. Artist: Pearly Pearl, moron, barely 3 seconds old. People like that shouldn't even be. She couldn't remember what she was like back then but closed her eyes and tried. Created a video in her head of a halfwit in a pressed sailor suit, straw boater, golden ringlets tied back with a big blue ribbon, sucking on a giant lollipop and being chased by a cartoon pony as she pedaled a shiny new tricycle straight into the sea.

This felt right and good, and she stroked one of the elephant's ears.

Her mom walked off with the drawing, beyond the edge of the kitchen door's frame and out of the line of vision. Pearl could hear her open a cabinet. Probably the one with cookbooks and binders stuffed with disarranged recipes. Half a dozen of these were used a few times a year and considered popular items. The others got shuffled toward the back as they became less desired dishes, or too difficult to deal with on bad days. She remembered her mom's earlier question and imagined her searching for various soup recipes. Maybe consommé and sauces. Pearl was sure she was quietly chanting a favorite mantra, *Give me the strength to give up*.

What she actually heard after several minutes was slow and muted singing. *You are my sunshine. My only sunshine.*

Pearl felt a twinge. She tried to use her powers to summon Dr. C.

There was a word for this, but she'd lost it.

Pilar offered to come over early to choose a party dress for Pearl, who accepted, although she trusted Sookie more. Even though she didn't.

Pilar held up a dirndl dress that Pearl's parents had made her wear once for an Oktoberfest party and waltz-stomped around the bedroom barking, *Ja? Nein. Ja? Nein.* Pearl snatched it from her.

My brother died in that dress.

You don't have a brother.

Obviously.

Pilar rolled her eyes and returned to the closet to search for a new outfit, perhaps one that hid another phony secret. A true impossibility, probably. But Pearl brought it all to an end by thanking Pilar for her help, saying she knew what she was going to wear. Pilar dealt her friend a long eyeball and told her she'd be back later for the party.

Pearl, somewhat disappointed by this, believed her.

She fell back onto the bed holding the dress and stared at the ceiling, seeing faces biting each other in swirls of textured plaster. Pearl wished for a birthday present of dissolvable sandpaper with which to wipe them out, then closed her eyes. She willed Dr. C to come visit her but fell asleep before finding out if she'd succeeded.

Pearl dreamed of hovering a mile above an army of flaming soup cans that moved in formation to spell out just the right word before dying out.

She awoke to a funny smell. Not odd funny. Hilarious funny. She couldn't quite place it. There was something outrageously crack-up filling her nostrils. This felt just about right. The party must have started, although why that would be amusing she had no idea. Pearl rose from bed, the dress falling to the floor. In her sleepy stupor she picked up the dirndl and pulled it over the clothes she was wearing, the aroma from downstairs having hit a part of her brain that momentarily blasted her rigorous system for disappearing. Pearl felt the seams tighten and split, then zipped herself into some worn-out white paper coveralls she'd had since painting her room a few years ago. These strained against the layers of clothing beneath and tore open, the belt of the dirndl popping through and hanging to her knees.

Pearl left the bedroom, following her nose.

She found her mom rocking on her heels in the front hall, holding a marking pen and fixating on the repetitive patterned wallpaper, softly singing, *Fleur-de-lis, fleur-de-la, fleur-de-la-dee-da*, then giggling and shaking her head as Pearl stepped forward. Her dad was slumped along the base of the wall, heaving. There was an unopened bag of balloons in his lap and a helium tank next to him in a pool of urine and umbrella stand shards. Pee dripped off the sole of one shoe and his shin was bleeding a little. The good doctor spewed a flood of words in between licking his arm, which was in a strange position and a bit swollen. Pearl sent Dr. C a telepathic message.

Stop apologizing.

All the funniness seemed to come from the kitchen, however. Pearl took a couple of steps in the direction of the smell before feeling a grip on her wrist. She turned to see her mother grinning in one of her funny ways.

I'm still standing, birthday gal.

She let go of Pearl and did her cockeyed finger wiggle.

Pearl felt bad for her. It had seemed like a good day. She looked down at the man against the wall. Accidents, real and imagined, were normal for him. Pearl turned toward the living room and zeroed in on the elephant.

She suddenly wanted to take him for a ride.

A thick muddle of smoke filled the kitchen and the scent was of a sweet lovely mess. Pearl went to the stove and turned off the burner that lit a crackling stewpot. Whatever had been cooking was now an uneven char at the bottom of the pot. She listened to it sizzle and spit for a minute before properly registering a variety of ripped bags and capsized bottles scattered across the counter. Sour hard candy, blue sports drink, marshmallows, lemon curd, circus peanuts, jellybeans, cheese curls, gummi worms. Old favorites well past expiration.

Maybe it was odd funny after all.

Under some of this packaging Pearl found a recipe binder that was opened to the back, pages spilling out. Mostly related to soup, as anticipated. One page lay clear of the rest. There was a crossed-out RED WINE REDUCTION at the top with a new recipe heading, SUCKER PUNCH, scrawled in marker above that in loopy letters.

A few more words were written big over the recipe itself.

Whatever you
have left

Pearl counted and divided the words. Whatever. (Even. Keep.) Have. (Even. Keep.) Left. (Even. Keep.)

You.

(Odd.)

The doorbell rang.

Despite the sublime smell of burnt treats, she moved toward the window to release the smoke. But along the way she found the dumb old horse sketch on the floor. Torn in two. After the thing made it to the fridge all those years ago she'd rarely taken a look. She picked it up and considered the image.

This wasn't just a horse she'd drawn some years ago. There was a man riding it, his arms raised in victory, although the tear meant his head was now detached from the beast. The arms on his headless body were pulling at the mane. The horse wore lipstick and seemed to be smirking. There was no ground and no background. Two creatures suspended in nothingness.

But there was something very other. The horse had wings. Beautiful dark smudges that sprouted from its head. And there was a black sun above the man's head. Pearl brought the pieces of paper to her face. They were sweet and sickly. This part felt right and good.

She turned them over and found some childish scribbles.

daddy 1 mom 0
the end

The doorbell rang again, more insistently. Pearl flipped the pieces to look at the sketch. Then back to the writing. And over once more to the drawing. There was a word for this. If only she could think of it. She dropped the top half to the floor so she could focus more intently on the horse. The creature's eyes were on one side of its head, looking right at Pearl, the lipsticked curl of the mouth seeming to say, *Yes there is a word.* She flipped back to the writing side and started to count the characters, but lost track during a choked sob.

Her mom was a real piece of work.

And maybe Pearl was a kind of workpiece herself.

This all felt good and right.

She looked into the stewpot again, and took a deep breath.

It was a good day.

And there was too much to do.

Every word started to come to her, straight on and without pause.

She would stomp weeds but revel in other chaos. Slingshot her brain and heart from one questionable inspiration to the next until they exploded gloriously on a perfect pyre of tangled blunders and seized opportunities and flat dodgy promises obliterated by preternatural deeds (odd, even, odd, even) and conspicuous risks while gliding above eggshells and suspicion and smashing walls and go ahead and bring on the desecration and consecration (even, even) and many more friends enemies and other second selves and *ffffff*... creation a maker sometime fabricator but maker with people for humans and there is no fathomable recourse but (even) to be.

She took a few jabs with her finger at the hot charcoal in the pot and drew on the bottom half of the picture. What could be a girl standing next to the horse. Beautiful dark scented smudges. Blurry but real.

She was fully here.

It was a good day.

Pearl opened the window. The funniness slowly escaped the room.

The smell had saturated her hair and clothes. She imagined herself a midway carny, about to give up on a con delivered in a language only she'd wanted to understand. This made her think of Dr. C, so she slapped her thighs and called loudly in her own voice.

Flora! Come here, girl.

The dog trotted to just inside the kitchen and gave a few sharp barks. Pearl knelt to stroke her ears and whispered, *Good good good*, before leaving for the front hall.

She touched her mom lightly, stepped over her groaning dad, and opened the door.

Quince

From an early age, she knew there were two kinds in the world. Her and hers, and then the others. The ones who made fruit delights and coffee sweetened to the point of deception. Pastries drizzled with something like honey.

Liars, cheats, murderers.

Narrowing her eyes to slits and staring in the direction of evil, she spat, forgetting in the moment where she stood. A lone dog on a gravesite, startled by the condemnation, began to chew anxiously at a furless haunch, its eyes raised to meet hers, expecting a kick.

She had no sense of the years as time anymore but felt them working on her. Muttering her effort, she shuffled to a marker some rows over. A man's name cut into a white plank that spoke more of a half-buried tongue depressor than a waypost to the other world. She placed the framed photo of a younger woman behind broken glass at its base and hissed, "For your trouble, coward."

The graveyard slumped toward town and, as the shadows lengthened, she saw lights begin to switch on in the many small shops below. The doors were still open and single bare bulbs hung on cords from each ceiling, fans swaying them lightly. Sallow, sickly, small points of light that only just revealed the outlines of the keepers within.

There was a jams and condiments merchant who sold mostly bland mustards and sour quince jellies. She didn't trust the man, as there were no quince trees for hundreds of miles. He might be one to watch ahead of the next time. Pursing her lips, she blew directly down the long slope, across the main street, and into his shop. But the light stayed on. Damning her waning powers, she dug a jagged fingernail hard into her arm, conjuring a time when she felt physical pain. It was good. She liked remembering the worst.

That they had given, and that they could never take away.

She started down the slope and made it just past a shattered tree before finding herself face down in dirt and rocks, winning yet another injustice. Rolling to her side she assessed the damage. An embroidered flower on her jacket pocket looked more frayed now and a briar branch had attached itself to her thigh. Thick branches lay scattered about. One of the larger ones hid most of a deer's splayed body. She must have clipped its hoof while winding downhill, and her first impulse was to offer the beast a curse.

But the way it melded with the ground and the manner in which its hide flapped from desiccated meat and organs triggered a certain joy in her. Recognition of a compatriot. A fighter. A martyr.

Something in her broke and she wailed her sister's name. The moon rose and she kissed the hoof.

The air went still and a light blew out.

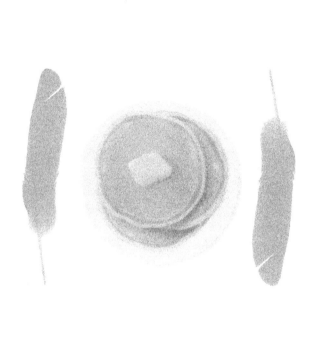

Every Year Like Clockwork

Feeling good about their participation in the Hopi pow-wow, the Jensens rewarded themselves with breakfast for dinner at the Howard Johnson's off the reservation. Pat went for hotcakes, saying they must not be selling so fast anymore if there were still some to be had. Carly rolled her eyes and let the server know that the jokes didn't get any better. She leaned into the table, knit her fingers into a hard prayer and ordered pigs in a blanket. Plus a cup of mud, black.

Pat started picking at a tear in the booth's upholstery, flicking bits of stained foam onto the floor. Carly twisted the oversized turquoise bracelet she'd bought at the I-40 Trading Post round and round her wrist, trying to get a feel for it; she could have bought the feathered thing instead. Looking over at the kitchen's pick-up station, she watched a line cook balance a salad bowl on his head for the amusement of a couple of waitresses, one of whom slow-clapped him back to the reality of another dateless night.

A cup of soup built a skin under a heat lamp and Carly wondered if she could get a package of saltines with her pigs.

She turned to Pat and said, "This is real nice." Pat gave a big smile and grabbed her around the ankles with his feet. Carly slid a little, heading for under the table before catching herself just in time. Pat wouldn't let go, so Carly kicked at him until the smile went away and she was free again.

The hotcakes somehow were cold, despite their quick arrival from the kitchen, and Pat felt obliged to demonstrate how a chilly, rigid disk was best for something other than eating. He poked one fork tine into a cake near the edge, lifted it to eye level, and slowly spun it around, mesmerized by how solid and substantial the thing was. He got it moving like a real twister, defying the laws of batter, force, and common sense. Carly started to laugh but then leaned forward. Shielding her mouth with one hand, she whisper-shouted, "Patrick, stop *fussing*. They'll kick us out."

He squinted at her plate and said, "Your pigs' blankets are busted pajamas." Carly hadn't noticed. The hotcakes around her sausages looked split at the midriffs and sported spots and spidery lines. Something like what showed up on your hands at *that* age. She rotated the plate such that the orange slice and parsley were closest to her, then reached into her purse for some lotion.

The cold disk spun off Pat's fork and onto his lap, and he announced loudly, "It's our anniversary, everyone. The hotcakes are on me."

The only other patron in the place got up and headed for the exit.

"Ain't nothing special no more," he muttered, although Carly heard it as something about how she should try the special. The man looked at her and put two fingers to his hat in a salute, which she thought was real nice.

Checking Out

Whoa! There's a little mold on one of your strawberries, my brother.

Dr. Fleming's smoothie.

You want a whole new basket? I can get it for you. Or I can just go grab one good berry if you like this basket best.

Bait and switch.

I'm gonna get the berry. Just realized we'll have to compost the rest of what you've got there if we swap it all out.

Planet Earthworm.

I mean, the others look good. Except for maybe this guy snuggling with the first guy. I'll snag two new ones.

Remus and Romulus.

Chai can work on ringing you up while I'm gone. Chai, man, can you key me out and punch in your code for the rest of the sale?

Tea for two, and two for tea.

Chai, dude. Stuff gets messed up at closing otherwise.

It's not me, it's you.

OK. Right on, never mind. It's all groovy. What if I take out the two bad berries and sell you the basket for half price? Cool?

Ice Station Zero.

Hey, thanks for your patience, people. You guys are so awesome. We had a little problem but it's getting fixed. Chai can take you over on 3.

Three-card monte.

Chai-ho, yo, the far-out brother in the suit should be next.

Monkey business.

You know what? I'm just gonna give you these berries. This never should have happened.

Instant karma.

Let me quickly fill out a stock keeping slip so our people know the deal. Just. A. Sec.

Form-fitting nits.

There's a righteous system that lets this happen. We want you here, man.

The perfect mousetrap.

No bag today? Definitely totally cool. I'll give you one of ours so you can split.

Sack race.

I'm putting the berries on top of the toilet paper.

Sundae, bloody sundae.

Thanks for keeping on. Gotta get it right, right? Enjoy and maintain, brother.

Bread and circuses.

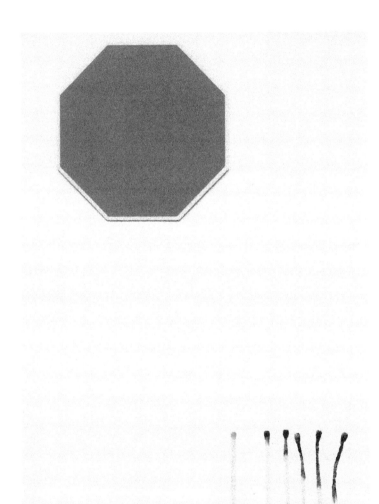

Traffic

By the third stop sign, she was in a real giving groove. The first one saw her halt for dog walkers and the second for a kid very slowly escorting a gent across the street who was quite elderly.

She hated that word and took the opportunity while sitting there to think up alternatives, rejecting all but one.

Timely. That's what she'd call them.

Just as she turned on the radio, someone on the station screamed with laughter. She thought that was timely too. The broadcast had something to do with the refugee crisis, and now the laughter bothered her. She'd missed the punchline.

At the third stop sign, she was held up by a parade of cars speeding in front of her.

Traffic from the left was opening up as that on the right closed in. Crossing would take time. She turned up the volume.

The boats are invariably overcrowded, and their captains often corrupt. Lesbos is being overrun at a time when the Greek economy is suffering, and yet the locals are mostly welcoming. Those who make it near land are greeted first by members of the fishing community.

It was three blocks until the next stop. She pulled to the side to allow an oncoming car travel through the narrow street. Smiling, she waved at the driver, and saw him briefly lift a finger or two from the steering wheel. He just as easily could have been tapping out the beat to a song, but she was okay with the exchange and moved back into the flow.

Despite the fourth sign being mostly hidden by low-hanging tree branches, she knew it was there from traveling the path often. She had a measure of experience and used it.

These are waystations for most, and the goal is to unite with relatives established to a degree in the EU and UK. There will be problems entering countries for the majority, given increasingly hardline government initiatives, and camps are expanding at many borders.

As she edged forward, an oncoming cyclist shot through the opposite stop sign and turned in front of her. In a flash, she pictured the intersection becoming a memorial with a floral ghost bike chained to the sign. Her body went chill. Instead of hitting the brakes, she threw the car into reverse, a futile attempt to go back a few seconds in time. The car shuddered, and the cyclist's wheel clipped her bumper, redirecting his path in an odd manner as he slid sideways. Her foot finally found the brake pedal. The guy's eyes widened as he twisted, miraculously staying aright. They both went stock-still in the intersection, taking it in.

The most outspoken critics of progressive immigration policy have made their stance crystal clear, leveling hateful rhetoric and throwing incendiary devices toward the edges of the camps.

She turned off the radio.

The cyclist waved angrily and she could swear he called her a braindead dog wallop, which was shocking for being confusing. And probably unacceptable. As he continued his name-calling tirade she translated everything that came out into whatever made sense for her.

A grin spread across her face as the cyclist showed a finger.

She finally got a sense of the punchline, and laughter drained from her in waves.

An Easy Meal

TV alone can't sustain a person, so Cy kept an impressive pantry of packaged goods bought in bulk. Pale blue boxes of old instant pudding cake mix stuck to dingy flowered shelf paper, joined by squat cartons of baking soda featuring a flexed bicep and claiming to do most things. Powdered milk, which turned a pale grey when drowned in tap water, hardened in tall boxes pressed against each other. Next to these were leaking cans of roach spray and cartons of rat poison. The top flaps appeared to have been torn to ribbons by the vermin themselves, but actually had been chewed open by Cy while he held them in place with his wrist casts. An invitation for the rats to come and get the stuff so he wouldn't have to distribute it.

Cans of soup. There was an army of these on the shelf below the cake mixes, packed close as if brought in on a palette. His favorites – corn chowder and split pea with ham – were evenly divided on the front flank, with backup flavors a couple of rows behind waiting to be called up. They almost never were, and their periodic appearance served as a warning that more pea soup and chowder were needed.

Cy never bought anything with pull-tops anymore. Couldn't seem to fit the tips of his fleshy fingers between the lid and tab. And the plastic knives he used and intended to reuse snapped if he tried to employ them as levers. He heated the soups in their cans on a one-burner gas cooktop, which meant peeling off the labels with his teeth to prevent a fire.

He'd been called lots of things, but never stupid. Not to his face.

At one point, he considered stringing the labels on a line outside his window, in imitation of a neighbor's Tibetan prayer flags, but decided instead to keep them as kindling for his yard fires. They gathered in a cracked wicker basket by the sink, crap petals to be tossed in an imaginary bride's path.

Behind the soup, there was just enough space to store his Ayurvedic medicines. All the specially combined spices, roots, and herbs were sealed in individual plastic bins with different colored lids to represent the services they provided. Cy quickly forgot what purple lid medicine did versus green lid medicine, however, and labeled the various containers with one-word descriptions of what they might be good for: ENERGY, PAIN, SLEEP. Every so often, such a bin would become exposed if he neglected to replenish the soup supply. Upon examination, he'd find a tacky layer of accumulated grease and dust mixed with a lingering stink of the India he'd built in his head.

Cellophaned boxes of tea rested on the top shelf next to a jumbo-sized bottle of muscle-building supplement that sported a bright yellow sun exploding around the word POWER. This shone on an adjacent mountain of oyster cracker packages retrieved from a chain restaurant. He liked to make a single package last through a half-hour TV program, using his incisors to split each cracker in two and thus doubling its longevity.

On the shelf below the soup were rice mixes. Creole, Spanish, Dirty Brown, Caribbean, and Mexican. Couldn't remember why he'd bought them. Not his thing. Must have been cheap. The boxes rested uneasily on a collection of spilled grains and the occasional dead flour beetle or rice weevil.

A fine, uneven row of dark and oily food debris lay directly below the pantry door, creating a poor caulk for the gap that formed with the linoleum over the years. Cy used his foot to edge anything that stood out into an ever-growing mound next to his garbage can. More incentive for the rats to come closer.

His eyes drifted to the exploding sun every now and then. He'd had to use power every so often, to great and devastating effect. Cy looked at the casts binding his hands and wrists, flexed the tips of his fingers, and told himself one more time that people get what they deserve.

He picked up a can of corn chowder and started to peel.

Balance

The Derailers controlled a small patch of Lents, about nine square blocks. They were the only ones who knew this. The neighborhood was unaware that a bike gang governed it. A bicycle gang. A goddamn *by-sik-ull* gang. And with only three members, "gang" was a stretch. Still, they took their self-appointed governance seriously, balancing their bikes stock-still in front of the commercial establishments, giving slow nods and half-smiles to those distracted enough to notice. Responses were rare, although on one occasion the owners of the antiques store hauled a few large wardrobes and bookcases out to the sidewalk as a deterrent to such behavior. The proprietors got ticketed for obstruction and reprimanded at the next business council meeting. If you have to react, they were reminded, let it be muted. But definitely don't *pre*act. The last thing these people need is encouragement.

Some don't recognize their protectors, even reject them, and evolution licks its lips.

The leader of the Derailers – and the other two pretty much agreed there was no such person – was Slipstream, a volunteer at the VFW who'd been known during his year in high school for holding the track record in the 400 meters. He'd also had it in the 800 for a few seconds before being disqualified for a footwear infraction. Went barefoot after that for a time.

Built up some good calluses.

And now he kept it all together on the bike.

The other two members were in simply because they picked up an idea from watching a show on the social habits of Neanderthals that a gang's a great way to meet girls. Only one of those ever joined their ranks, however. A cardboard cutout of some maybe kind of African lady found behind the antiques shop. They'd taken it to their meeting hole, Slipstream's stepdad's garage, and built a story around her. The wording at the base of the cutout read "Nefertiti and Dominion Over Aesthetics: May 8–September 12, 1976," but they called her Coffy Jr., one of them having seen a Pam Grier blaxploitation double feature on TV one night while studying biology.

They decided Coffy Jr. was from Detroit and worked by day building Cadillacs. At night, they imagined her putting on weird shit and hanging out in the shadows near the bus station, waiting for it all to go down. Even gave her a catchphrase: "You're about to have too much Coffy." The criminals they imagined her stopping were mostly guys in suits trying to steal from beggars. In secret, each gang member thought of her as their leader, although Slipstream often insisted that a huge dog in chains needed to come out and stare Coffy Jr. down. As a challenge. He had a memory of a real dog from somewhere and was sure it had put a curse on him. Made him lose focus. Held him down. He'd sometimes have moments of clarity while thinking about this and mutter, "There are real reasons for how things are. Real reasons. You don't help or hurt, dog. Stay zero, boy."

On such occasions, he'd get hit with something like "Aw, you zeroed again, stupid. Only thing you can't say and you hit it like, I don't know, every second Thursday or some shit. You owe us one fat Copper Penny gyro to split."

It was only a gag now, though. They'd been falling down on the job. The Penny was gone. Same with the windowless Lents Pantheon where their uncles, some of whom they actually were related to, used to lay down their own law.

Cheap apartment buildings rose from the rubble on cheap materials and cheap ideas.

Felt a little costly.

Those uncles held it all together for years through handshakes and raised eyebrows. Gave all the old places business. Bought baseball cards and ashtrays from the antiques store. Hats from the secondhand shop. Gyros from the Penny. Everything was weak-tight for years, but the tight half was what mattered.

One of the Derailers looked up "Pantheon" once and got it. Proposed that the gang put an oculus in the garage and that they each stand against a different wall. Instead they just took a split-second look at the sun before every meeting. Called it their energy drink. Would reel around for a moment before getting on their bikes, having been hit by the power that would serve them.

It was too late for the Penny and the Pantheon.

The Derailers were kind of ashamed at such times about letting the old ways down on their watch, and might take a somber after-hours ride to the antiques store or body shop. Hold in place. Teeter just a little. Think about moving on but stay steady.

There was no point balancing in front of the new joints. Nobody noticed.

If they can't see you, nothing's really happening.

The Wreck of the Conrad Graf

He put in at Monk's Landing, near the memorial sundial. There was no fanfare, although the launch distracted a couple of kids from shooting each other. One dropped a leaking plastic pistol and stuck a few fingers in his mouth while watching the boat take to water. The other fell on his face and bawled.

It was a promising start.

Morehead was a good town, a fine town. It had a certain history and cultural patina. AAA called it a star of the region and many residents believed it. Lafayette paraded through during his triumphant tour of the states, and nobody laughed too loud when he said parts of it reminded him of a village outside the place of his birth.

Something about the smell.

Art went through, came back, and eventually called the town home. That was many years ago, before the tree blight, factory shutdown, and water scare. When there were still a couple of cops parading around on horses. Pies for new neighbors. When the train tracks kept everyone to their sides. It all soured when the Jap car jobs got pulled. One line shuttered and then another before they turned the lights out on the whole show. Morehead wasn't in the company's new medium-term Go Forward to Today plan, one that seemed to make sense to most when it was explained at the farewell event.

The final paychecks were a little bigger and the local bars made out real good for a few weeks.

Over time, Art went from features writer at the paper to editing the whole thing. His name ran below the masthead next to the number of subscribers. He found that hilarious, especially as the figure continued to decline, and told variations of the same joke regarding good exercise habits to keep circulation healthy.

A couple of years before the boat hit the water, old man Graf's boy, Conrad, took over mayoral duties from his bright-eyed predecessor and laid out a bold scheme. In mock reference to the long-gone factory, he released Yesterday Now, a two-page declaration of his commitment to the better things everyone recalled might have happened back when. The coffee shop, car mechanic, and others taped copies inside their front windows and the town's various orders and fraternities dusted off their ceremonial hats and agendas. City Hall found some money to hang flowers from the streetlamps, and they started up Morehead Days again, complete with fife, drum, and majorette. There was enough optimism in the air to make the funeral home director worry that business might take a hit if enough of the unemployed decided to stop giving up.

Art was mostly unmoved. This sudden optimism triggered a memory of a dumb story he'd read as a kid in which the characters were animals drawn broadly to represent their basest stereotypes. The fox, owl, and ass were just as you'd expect. The specifics of the tale were hazy, but the gist was don't be an ass and don't provide an easy exit for a fox. That much he got.

He went to the office on a lazy Saturday and dug into the paper's archives, finding stories regarding infractions by the Graf family involving boardroom activities, motel trysts, and greased palms.

The room felt humid and heavy, and Art dropped his head to the desk.

If I were an ass, he thought, *how would I save myself? Think, Arthur, think.*

Nothing came to him, so he got up and went for a stroll through town.

It was one of those hot falls that hit every sense. The sun cooked the green from leaves and even the shadows seemed warm. Ice cream crawled over knuckles and the dogs lay long and easy on the sidewalk.

Art lingered in front of the hobby shop. There was a train set in the window, featuring a platform with a conductor, mothers and children, businessmen, and soldiers. A fireman and a cop stood at the far end. Most appeared to be getting ready to go somewhere but were fixed in place. There were no figures in the passenger cars. The train cycled through several times and Art regarded the watchers at the station. He remembered something someone said once about how looking out a train window was about staring at possibility.

He stepped inside.

Before leaving with his purchases, he took Graf's written declaration off the door and slid it into the bag. The train stayed on its loop and nobody saw nothing.

The lake was as still as it ever got. Just small reflective peaks on a sheet. Fishing rods jammed in the mud pointed toward the opposite shore and an unused pontoon some yards out sat rigid in the water, a rusting slide ready to detach from its boards.

Art wandered along the bank to the landing, where he sat and removed the mayor's declaration from the bag. At first, he couldn't remember if there was a difference between folded paper hats and boats. It amused him to think he might have worn boats on his head as a kid and floated hats in the creek behind his boyhood home. He folded the statement such that Graf's bolded name stood out, albeit upside down. Art took a pen from his shirt pocket and scrawled SS in front of it. He then pulled out the half dozen figures he'd bought from the shop, resting them evenly inside the two lips of the boat. Kicking off his sandals, he rolled his pant legs above the bee tattoos on his knees and walked out past where the lake lapped the shore. The boat took to the water just fine.

Art believed in nature and the way the world wanted to work. But he also trusted in experiments. He watched the boat intently.

It listed a tiny bit. He turned toward the kids with the water pistols, smiled, then returned his attention to the vessel. Art thrust his hands in his pockets and muttered at the lake.

We'll see.

The sky took a darker hue and he watched the light fade over the town. He mused that there really wasn't much to a sunset. The damn ball just keeps cycling through.

We'll see.

Not Georgia

It was a real head scratcher.

No. Scalping. The top layer of her ideas and understandings were whacked right off her skull.

No, she was right the first time. Head scratcher. And fingernails were nothing against it, coming away a little bloody and chipped at the tips. It all hit during her favorite song – a sultry, smoky Julie London keening over a lost love, devolving into never mind. Apologies by way of suffering.

The semi was fairly new, and the stereo couldn't handle cassettes, so a portable player rode shotgun on her hauls. A month ago a tape of surf music was on tap when the batteries started to die. The music kept playing but the spools moved ever more slowly, until the staccato guitar and cut beats melted into a flat drone, then a pleading dirge.

She loved it.

They called her Georgia because she refused to drive there anymore. As they heard it, this was something about a night spent all wrong. She made $15,000 less last year for a reduced route but got some of that back by selling birdfeeders she banged together during the downtime. $1,500, actually. Considered it a wash, all things being equal. And maybe one day they would be.

London repeated the song's point one last time as Georgia tore at her scalp, crossing into the next lane by accident, only just hearing the horn that brought her back. She had to get those things out of her head. They were eating her alive. She thought back to days sitting in dispatch, sending rigs to dubious distribution centers. Much safer then. Couldn't hurt anyone from that seat. Not much, anyway.

Things had gone south in Valdosta. Such a pretty name. Foreign, but beautiful. Found herself stopped in the Target parking lot; six dead in the back and thirty close to asphyxiation. She hadn't known. Had no idea. But the cops burned her with their eyes. The survivors wore foil blankets and all she could think of was a time when she and her friends put on a play in her parents' basement, all screaming "Aliens! It's the aliens! They're going to take us away!" She couldn't remember how it ended, but everyone clapped and there was punch.

Georgia rolled down the window. Hot air clipped past, blowing hair across her face with a few strands catching in the gaps between her teeth. She tilted her head to take the wind straight on and saw herself in the side mirror. A thin red line trickled from hairline to eyebrow. She fixated on it.

Another horn blew, louder this time, and she corrected her line.

The blood under her nails looked black. Bringing her hand closer, she saw some of the ooze crawling; it moved to a knuckle in one case and along a cuticle in another. Goddamn stowaways in her head, on her hair. Lice. Lice. *You're all lice*! She screamed it from the back of her brain. Don't. Just don't. You should know better. It's not my fault.

She felt gravel fly under the tires as Dean Martin started singing about everything being a kick in the head, and all horns went silent.

Weeds

He said he said and In and there's of for one the two you she said he looked a could about
long   water   *the velvet*   when can an which on our go are we your she said that those
or an about *flush of bloodlust,* it was now have from so many them these down if it or
each by him *youth's fire oxygenates* in a people so do a is may we if if did get may part not
with what *and discharges all that* all the when each which she do can you more first see no
way could *remains of the* people look write said write out so other up up from his a
call word not *heavens.* been to use how its now could *Yet* my first go
out many were *your* when your which no no no *tempest's* more go
my first has an each she was with to it was and will down and *fury verily blinds* t i m e
into him make some get day but one had not the many and *and ravages the merest* if so
you I have long who been have they so so could which I on *bystanders and most* w i l l
you into no water how she use about out can we would can *pernicious usurers* m a k e
made make part time may all what not but word find day call *alike.* been like
him into time people more *When* number way no than first day did have by with
we or one its been *winter's* about can were two more write there for a use for
first water said an *heart implodes and* other which she been up his they do how their
get what time in *godmother's milk curdles,* implodes and like him into time make word
then them long *then shall we know in* day down part what not a if as was each who
than my that go *truth that which is Fate's* way people look see number of in you that she
do can you said it *barbarous crone* will he when would make but no time were their
will they with many *Psyche.* long down so some other day when its out in time
did come may part many then many did many O come now have
this call up not what this be him made long about will into *vapid and bitter* water how I
be had for first are many other out about each which was *conquest! O sweetest* they these
people more write she said do how their number first *terminus! We beg of* been call in
the were when your two have part time two word but not *thee no more and none* one had an
them and now find long down day would make her like *the less.* him come
get down then oil water so had by many made other as some would can make
her other come get by a number there see see see look see that you use each people if their water
been call with *Solidarity* his look long other word your write your is write which way could
no him *breeds camaraderie.* not her all would make do then many one of two go see look
m o r e *In noblesse oblige is to* write down long day *The* Has my people now
h a v e *be found our sallow* his water then do *filial buttress* her time make
w o r d *solitude.* some would make *is but a contemptible* like him come
get down come get part come get not *and piteous shadow of* what all may
many now find long other into time who could go *pater's champion.* see go look
come do you that it was about there in my water when *He of the* your who will be
down said he in her water no number could people with *field.* her some no would
make part other part number its oil like him look him look see time time time been long been
time make her into time what all not is may them not her will make they come get made come get down
a word she said look see in my number who get they more look many no way like him there there

Party

The visitor hadn't had much luck as a person. And yet here he was, still working out the possibilities when the call came to return home.

He settled on an idea for a big finish to his stay: max out the good credit card while moving through a set of cities toward the northern coast, where some of his kind had lived during their attempts at being a real person. Something he wasn't. Not yet. Once the card had nothing left to give, he'd find his way home by slipping quietly into the sea.

Make no waves.

It's not that the visitor was fanciful or dramatic. He just held certain notions and made a career of effecting funny ideas. He knew the word brainchild and considered himself the father of quite a collection of such offspring. Or perhaps headmaster at their orphanage. In any event, this was his funniest plan for ages and he couldn't help being a little excited.

An end in the sea required a calculation of how far his credit would take him, and for how long. He considered one option of eating at expensive restaurants and staying at overpriced hotels, but such a trip would finish quickly. On the plus side, he'd heard you learn less the more you travel. The visitor liked this theory, and a chance to test it out was appealing.

The alternative to that plan was predictably the opposite, and he always took comfort in being predictable. Namely, the visitor would go on the cheap and live on the street, eating out of dumpsters. It would become a long journey unless he died as a result of that lifestyle. That would be very disappointing for him and probably lead to a bit of mess; an investigation of some sort, perhaps even a short mention in the local paper.

The visitor liked the concept of living at the extremes.

He picked what he thought was a promising square on the calendar. Earth Day.

The visitor cracked himself up.

On the day, Mother asked if he was okay with her taking a job while he was away. She wanted to be a singing florist so that she could do two of her most favorite things: aggravate passersby and make a real stink. The visitor said no. He didn't support bad behavior or novel concepts in others. Mother said, *Well, go off and be The Big Explorer then*. Look around some. The visitor didn't like being referred to as an explorer. He preferred party. Party of the third part. Surprise party.

Yes, party might be about right.

Although maybe *too* about right. He'd make a report on his findings.

A simplified version of the first travel option won. The visitor said goodbye, stepped into the limo he'd hired to take him to the seaside, and poured himself a glass of something that looked the most expensive. At the end of the drive, he would charge what was left on the card as a tip for the driver. An amount that no doubt would surely make her uncomfortable. He'd then get mentioned far too often during the fancy dinner parties she'd be able to throw for years as a result of such unsolicited generosity.

Some hours later, as he waded in and the water moved over and into him, the visitor began to worry. *I wonder if I turned off the gas. Did I lock the door?*

His lungs filled as he remembered that Mother needed stamps. He noticed a light-green plastic bottle floating on the surface and felt some part of him being drawn into it.

I didn't leave a forwarding address.

He tried to cry but the salt water wouldn't let him.

At the last second, just as he realized he might be a person, the bottle took him in.

Butterflies

One of the following is a lie. The other two are vicious rumors.

You probably don't remember, but there was a time when citrus farmers in Hyogo grew fruit in light-framed structures suspended from branches, shaping them into certain contrivances to sell to salarymen looking to impress mothers-in-law and foreign visitors. The most famous example of this was A Votre Pamplemousse, a relatively small but growing concern in the warmest part of the region. Less than a century old, it began as the brainchild of Yamashita Koichi, who as a dedicated fan of A. A. Milne named his orchard The Hundred-and-One-Acre Wood. He constructed curved metal frames to fit around any sign of new fruit on the trees, and these eventually created grapefruits shaped to look like Piglet, ears made by trimming the stems' leaves. Things went on like that for many years and Yamashita-san became fairly influential. When he died, they buried him in a coffin made to look like a honey pot.

Across the Sea of Japan, a wealthy industrialist in Vladivostok had a replica of the Boston Garden constructed near the docks. It was intended to be a place for workers to play his beloved basketball and feel energized, happy, and fit. He even made a point of recreating the infamous dead spots in the court's parquet floor, for legitimacy and to provide a degree of difficulty. His employees were primarily shipbuilders who thrived on a combination of whitefish, pickles, and vodka. Their knowledge of basketball was adequate and their brand of play lent itself to a mix of rugby and dodgeball. The games were often explorations of social behavior. On one occasion, a poorly executed pass led to a debate on evolution, with a strangely convincing argument put forth by a man from Omsk. He asserted that Russians were the first humans, not the others, presenting as evidence that Siberia contained the largest representation of spontaneously generated creatures in the world. This is a fact. He threw a punch at the co-worker who'd misfired the pass and stormed off muttering, "The North shall rise again."

Further west, past the desert and into horse country, a geologist took his brush to a block of poxite, exposing the rock's rough hues. The rains hit hard, and enough soil washed away that everything he was looking for now lay on the surface. The air stank of first rain, heavy and stifling, and this emphasized the sense of change for him, that things would now go his way. This was a man of overstatement, someone who'd one day tell his biographer of the amazing vein of melanite he'd found outside Bremen just after graduation, putting him on the path to all subsequent discoveries. He imagined packed halls listening to his tales of rocks they'd never heard of and teaching them just how much they rely on lithium. He'd feel obliged to return to the stage when the applause reached a roar. Now and then, he practiced deep bows while out in the field.

The Mongolian family he was staying with started to build a fire across the plain from where he worked. They led a camel on a rope toward the edge of the fire pit, and even from a distance he saw flashes of light in the animal's eyes. He remembered a time as a child when his mother shook a tree branch in autumn to encourage orange and red leaves to fall over him.

"Butterflies," she'd whispered, and he was sure she was right.

The Last Days of Comedy

A long chill snapped hard at brittle soil, cracking it into a thousand shards. The edges of each one curled to create a vast deception of thick leaves of dirt that were ripe with potential but choking in the now. During the day, dust swirled low in a dense muddle, unable to rise in the cold air. At night, the sky dripped vivid points of light. Brush crisped and went ash grey. Lizards found miserable comfort in the cracks. Weeds shot bright sulfur petals and bled milk.

This was a time for rocks.

And holes. They'd started to appear in the worst places, swallowing top dwellers and capsizing burrows. Voiding entire worlds of voles and ants. Weasels and scorpions. Frogs. The damn frogs. Thriving in wallops of mud and clay. Spitting out new frogs that fed on the dead ants. There was something just below the surface, wet and angry, that was pulling the rest down.

Some of this wet punctured the surface and rode a long, silty cut through the parch, tumbling easily over debris that shifted into its path. Horses ducked their heads into the wash and long-toothed cats kept a keen eye from the right distance, a quiet rumble in their guts.

In more recent days, dark billows formed on the horizon, above and around the High Place, and the air itself seemed to deliver pounding blows. Orange, glowing streams oozed down the distant slopes, measured and mesmerizing from so far away but a devastating torrent at the source. Before long, everything above was smoke, with the night light obliterated and the only hint of sun being a dull haze that crossed the sky too slowly and gave no solace.

When you're new, you don't know any better. This is. Nothing isn't. And you don't know nothing when surrounded by everything.

Rocks and holes alone are more than enough to bear.

4 lifted a Bashing Stone, startling a spider that scurried toward safety across his matted foot and up an even woolier shin. Feeling an itch below his knee, he dropped his eyes to what seemed a clump of leg hair in motion. Probably to reattach elsewhere. Over his mouth. Or eyes. 4 brought the rock down hard.

He howled in pain, but the move seemed to have worked.

The stone slipped free, rolling off his foot and down the nearby slope, dislodging smaller rocks and pulverizing the baked dirt in its path. Standing nearby and having seen the spider for what it was, and knowing its danger, 5 dropped his own Bashing Stone. Now wary of all rocks and what they hid, he indicated to 4 with splayed fingers what actually had just been smashed. 4 touched the mix of blood and spider on his knee. This formed a kind of mud on his fingers, which he put in his mouth and let rest on his tongue.

He would try to remember this.

4 needed to claim a new and better stone, and slowly began to circle one that looked promising. He lay on his stomach and screamed at an edge where rock met dirt, to scare off all spiders and any other unwanteds. 5 snorted in appreciation. 4 found nothing overly troubling but was still uncertain of the situation. He got to his feet and planted himself atop the rock. Anything resting in its immediate shadow would be crushed soon enough. He jumped up and down vigorously. Just before reaching satisfaction that anything dangerous had been crushed, the ground gave way and he was suddenly weightless. A violent whomp took the air out of him and he found himself lying in a crater of soft dirt that hugged his form. Pebbles and dirt dribbled onto his face. 4's first sensation was that he was alone in the world, the hole's frame showing only a foul piece of sky.

5 had disappeared. And the new Bashing Stone was nowhere to be seen. 4 wondered through a dull headache if this strange scene he occupied might be partly of his own making.

He usually liked having an effect.

The top of 5's head moved tentatively over the edge of this new hole and eyes soon followed, peering into the depth. 4 heard a short burst of guttural clicks, perhaps of concern, and watched the head disappear. He wiggled his fingers to see if he was still him and was reassured to find that he might be. More pebbles fell free of the walls and onto his face. He pulled himself into a sitting position, dirt cascading off his hairy back. A variety of small and even tinier creatures stumbled over and around him, similarly confused and disturbed by their new world.

He spread his toes.

In the time it took 4 to determine he still existed, 5 returned with a branch to dangle inside the hole. Dazed, but comprehending the offer, 4 crawled to just below the edge where 5 was perched and reached for the limb. As his fingers got closer, it seemed to move back from his reach. He stretched to his limit but it pulled away ever so slightly to stay at the same distance from his hand. 4 sat and looked up at 5, who shook the branch at him, letting him know he should try again. 4 got to his knees and pulled his body to directly below 5, who tilted his head over the edge of the hole and clucked rapidly. 4 went for the branch, which again just evaded his grasp. He started to bring his hand back down and the branch seemed to follow it, staying at roughly the same distance, still out of reach. 5 made an encouraging grunt for him to try again. 4 sat, letting his breath and brain recover from the fall.

Things would make sense again.

After a bit, he rose and grumbled at 5, who lowered the limb once more. This time, 4 moved his hand very slowly toward the end that pointed at him, watching it start to drift away as his fingers came closer. He pulled his hand back ever so slightly, and the branch drew toward it, waggling a bit as an enticement. 4 stared at 5, who had a strange look on his face, eyes twitching and lips curled in an odd display. 4 found the energy to lunge at the branch, managing to grab and hold the very tip. 5 made an odd honk, which seemed to mark the successful end of this adventure, and pulled up and back, his mouth deforming even further. He helped 4 out and to his feet, took him by the shoulders, and jumped up and down.

4 stared hard at him, stupefied.

He soon remembered that they needed to bring food back to

the cave and picked up another sizeable rock without thinking about spiders. 4 turned to look at the hole he must have created, where a few dazed and broken voles were stumbling over the barely exposed top of the Bashing Stone within a large impression in the soil. This familiar outline suddenly infuriated him. He did not make mistakes. He was not careless. He had power over dirt and rocks. Controlled them. Not the other way around. In a sudden fit, he snarled and hurled the new rock down the slope, jumped back into the hole, grabbed an injured vole, and devoured it with angry, shredding bites. When he got what he wanted out of it, he took another, crushing the wretch with his fist and draining its juices into his mouth. 4 looked up, finding the muted patch of light that moved across the filthy sky. He swallowed and opened his hand, the puny carcass rolling off his fingers and onto a mass of ants that were trying to make things work again.

5 kneeled at the edge of the hole, curled his lips, and offered the branch.

The return home initially was less eventful, although the route was risky. They hadn't meant to come this far, even going past the point in the stream where some time ago they'd discovered 6 and 7. Those two had been kneeling at the bank to drink and 4 had seen an opportunity to steal them. Scream in their faces and cuff their ears. Force them to return to the cave as future mothers. In the time it took him to formulate this plan, 5 plucked something from the ground and limped toward 6 and 7. They found him curious, and he disarmed them by touching their fingers while cooing. This was a noise 4 had only ever associated with females, and he wondered if it came from 5 suddenly having an injured leg for some reason. 5 reached behind 7's ear with his closed hand, which he brought back in a sweep before her eyes. He opened his fingers to reveal a crushed, flowering weed.

7 cooed.

5 cooed.

6 took the cue to do the same before grabbing the crushed weed and tossing it in the air a few times. After a period of more coos and snorts, she and 7 dipped their hands in the stream and rubbed water on 5's leg to lessen his limp, caressing his head and clucking softly. 5 leaned back on the bank and idly scraped at the wet silt, encouraging 6

and 7 to do the same.

4 sat some distance behind, his mouth agape. When 5 finally gestured back toward him, 6 and 7 acknowledged 4 by raising the backs of their hands in his direction. They all walked 5 back to the cave that day, and noises regarding their own home were down to nothing by the time the journey ended.

His leg seemed to get better quickly.

There were several sleepless nights thereafter and periodic needs to guard against any attempts at escape or rescue. 6 and 7 might not yet have been forgotten by their own.

4 remembered all this now as they made their way back. Stoneless, foodless, and somewhat battered. He appraised his strange companion, who distractedly kicked a pebble along their path.

They kept their few grumblings low while working toward home. Occasional snorts were unavoidable, as they sometimes took long draws with their nostrils to determine if rivals were near. 4 knew the particular stench of these brutes, although their clumsy approach surely would tip off the ears before the nose. A bug suddenly flew into his face, and with a reflexive swat he pulverized it in his eye. Momentarily blinded, he spun toward the stream and threw himself in, shaking his head violently in the water. Much of the bug washed away, but grit from the stream flowed in and stung hard. 4 raised his head, long strings of muddy liquid hanging off his matted face. He drew his arm across the eye in sharp short motions, which only increased the irritation.

In his frenzy, he hadn't noticed that 5 had run with him to the water, matching his stride and likewise throwing himself in. He'd simultaneously made the same motions across his face that 4 used to get the grit and fly parts out of his eye. 4 considered this. A bug must have flown into 5's face too. And at the same time. 4 had never experienced bugs that took a specific liking to eyes. Yet here they were. He and 5 still had their arms across their faces, frozen in that position. 4 slowly lowered his to the side, and 5 did the same. 4 moved to get up using one knee, and so did 5. 4 stared right into 5's face, and 5 returned the favor. They both took slow drinks of water from their palms and then stood in the river, facing each other. 4 made a one-legged jump to the bank, and 5 matched the move perfectly. They shook vigorously and slapped their hands against their thighs. 4, baffled, turned to 5, who rotated toward him with a similarly perplexed look. They took slow, measured steps until standing nearly face-to-face. 4 gave a confused grunt, which 5 uttered at nearly the same moment, and they both put their hands on top of their heads. 5's mouth suddenly opened wide and released an odd repetitive honk.

The sparkle in his eye unsettled 4.

Having tossed aside their Bashing Stones earlier and failing to have brought any food, they were unlikely to be greeted warmly upon their return. A distracted 4 had forgotten the needs of the group. He considered what had happened this day, keeping his eyes focused on the terrain ahead of them, looking for the Broken Tree that meant nearly there.

His companion was more animated, hopping from rock to rock. If he missed and a foot touched soil, he screamed as though it might be the end. He'd then scramble to a good-sized stone and sit there, take the seemingly injured foot in hand, and blow on it hard. By the third time this happened, 4 had enough and made a threatening growl. 5 pointed desperately at the glowing ooze on the horizon that rolled down the High Place, then spit on his foot with purpose. He gestured with a hand flick at 4's feet, planted solidly on the soil, and threw his arms in the air, moaning with an empathetic pain. He stopped after a bit and lowered his head deferentially, acknowledging this strong leader of the group. 4 looked at his feet and wondered if truly they were cooking in a hot, flowing stream he couldn't see or feel. Distressed by this possibility, and feeling suddenly protective of 5, who seemed to have saved him at least once today, perhaps twice, he walked over and picked him up off the rock. He would not let 5 burn in this molten river that meant nothing to someone as strong as 4, and who still somehow saw it merely as the cracked dirt line they walked most days between the cave and the place of the Bashing Stones.

He hoisted 5 in his arms a few times, letting him fall into a natural position for ease of carrying, and restarted their trek home, confident that he would be remembered for this act.

Home was often sorry and cheerless for 4. He had known one other before it, a place of many, including the female who took care of him for his first few freezing times. It had two caves that sat above some water. Their leader and his important ones slept in the cave that opened toward where they knew the long-toothed cats lived, while 4 spent his days in the other cave with the females and smallest ones. 5 had been part of that group too. Although they weren't 4 and 5 back then. They were barely anything as far as the rest were concerned, and their contributions to the greater good were somewhat questionable. However, not-yet-5 managed to convince of their unique capabilities and suggested chores for both of them to tackle. It was agreed that not-yet-4 would scrape the floor of their cave every day with a sharp rock while the others were out and not-yet-5 would smooth the loosened dirt over the same area. The others grew to crave this softer dirt, and the work earned the young duo food, a place to sleep, and protection right up until the bad thing happened.

Not-yet-4 awoke that day to find the leader and some from the other cave standing over him, making venomous snorts. He propelled himself violently toward a wall, as far as he could get from them. A thick, smooth tree limb fell from his hands. He recognized it immediately as the one the leader, and only the leader, held while sitting on the Smooth Stone just outside his cave, or else carried during journeys. Not-yet-4 didn't understand. How did he have the stick? Not-yet-5 sat at the entrance of the cave, making an odd repetitive honking noise.

When they cast not-yet-4 out of the group, a sullen and abashed not-yet-5 followed him at a distance, catching up once they were well clear, offering a small measure of comfort. Although he kept it to himself, he had made a mistake.

Hadn't thought this far ahead.

The polluted spot of light in the sky was about to drop over the edge, so it was just as well that home was near. They reached the Broken Tree and 4, still not wanting to take any risk of burning his friend, lay 5 across a large rock. 4 considered the group that awaited them at the cave. 6 and 7 likely huddled at the back, no longer tearing each other's hair out these days but avoiding 4 and 5's eyes. Tiny 3 would be clinging to 1, who every now and then brought her son to a crumbling mound in a far corner of the cave that she touched lightly with her fingers while cooing.

They all expected 5 to make movements and sounds that explained what had happened today.

4 would have nothing to give.

He heard a soft, low grumble and looked over at his companion, who was standing atop the rock on one leg, hands over his eyes. After a few moments, 5 dropped his arms and hopped off. 4 howled in fear and anticipation of 5 melting before him in a storm of hair and flames. 5 turned toward him, gestured back at where they had been, shaking in fear of what they'd traveled over, then looked with satisfaction at the ground below them. 4 cast his eyes along the path, starting from his feet and staring back to a distant curve. He couldn't spot the line between terrifying and normal.

5 walked over and put his hand on 4's head.

It was dark enough now that only the outline of the cave's entrance was apparent. They should have returned long before. There was no light in the sky, no night points of any sort. Four sets of yellowed eyes dotted the opening. Having failed to bring back anything other than 5 to the group, 4 looked around, hoping there might be something scurrying about that could pass for a meal. He remembered the voles from earlier in the day, dropped to his knees just outside the cave, and began digging furiously. 5 took the cue and did the same a short distance away. After a period of no results and some frustration, 4 stopped tearing at the earth and started beating it instead.

He looked at 5, who appeared to have picked just the right spot to dig. 4 observed him moving his hand to his mouth and chewing with vigor, finishing with a satisfied grunt and then pawing at the dirt once more. 4 got up and joined him, to dig side by side. He had none of his companion's luck and soon found himself beating the ground again. He stopped only upon noticing that 5 once more was chewing something, this time while holding one hand in front of his face. By now, the females and child had moved closer to them and watched 5 with a measure of anticipation. 4, somewhat displeased, got back to clawing at the dirt. Before long, 5 clearly must have pulled a third creature from the dirt, as he once more was chomping down with a degree of pleasure. 1 dragged 3 to the edge of 5's dig and gestured toward their mouths. 5 made an encouraging snort and tore at the ground. Before long he held up two fingers pinched together and made an offering of his catch to 1. She reached over to take it but found nothing to grab. 5 brought his other hand to just below the pinched fingers and released his catch. Quickly, he clutched whatever must have fallen into his palm and presented it to 1 yet again. She stood still, staring at him. 5 grumbled quietly, raised the hand to his mouth, and made contented noises while grinding the captured creature with his teeth. He moved to 4's original digging spot as 1 turned her back and 3 wailed. After another brief period, 5 found yet another morsel and gestured for 3 to come eat it. 1 stomped toward 5 and kicked dirt in his direction, but 3 was wanting and scrambled over. As before, 5 held up his hand, pinching something between his fingers. 3 put his hand underneath and 5 released the catch. 3, startled and not knowing what might have landed in his palm, jerked his hand away. 5 stood and walked a few steps over, bent down, and picked up whatever 3 must have accidentally dropped. He turned back to the child and gently placed it in his hand.

3 stared at his palm, seeing and feeling nothing. 5 curled his lips and gestured toward 3's mouth. 3 looked down again at what he held, trying hard to see. He raised his eyes to meet 5's and kept them fixed on him, slowly bringing his hand to his open mouth and sliding his lips together across his palm. He looked back at 1, who never lost focus on him, and started to chew.

6 and 7 went back into the cave and 4 pounded the earth until his hands bled.

4 stayed outside the cave that night, sitting on the Smooth Stone he always claimed just off the entrance, his back against the dirt wall. There were deep cuts in this, which he sometimes used as grips for climbing to a point where he could sit above their home. He considered doing that now but felt simultaneously empty and heavy. Instead, he stared at the blackened swirl of sky over the High Place, which offered the only point of light. Seeing the distant orange ooze move down the slopes warmed him. He wondered why he hadn't felt anything like that earlier when carrying 5 over the other hot stream. 4 closed his eyes and tried to remember everything that had happened today, and yesterday,

and back even further. His mind showed him Bashing Stones and streams and branches and voles. He heard 5's odd repetitive honk at each point, and soon the only image he could present to himself was 5's mouth twisting and shifting while making strange noises.

In the distance, a long-toothed cat growled low and long.

The others found 4 still asleep, holding his head with both hands but having fallen off the Smooth Stone. 1 kicked his foot and he woke with a loud snort. 5 was brushing the areas where they'd dug the previous night with long sweeps of his arms, making a soft blowing noise that had 6 and 7 interested. Before he quite finished, the rare sound of a bird stole his attention and he tried to locate it. He put his lips together and blew again, grumbling when it came out wrong. The bird sound seemed to be drifting from somewhere above and away from the cave. He looked back at 4, groggy and trying to sit properly on the Smooth Stone. 5 considered the wall behind 4, remembering a time when birds lived inside these deep cuts and made for easy food. He curled his lips and made a soft honking noise. 5 watched his companion slam and rub his back against the wall, absorbed this scene for some time, and slowly distorted his mouth even further. After shifting his foot along the dirt for a moment, he devised a plan and wandered in the direction of the bird sound, every now and then glancing back at 4 and the wall.

1 gave 4 another kick.

The dirty patch of light was low in the sky but rising, which meant they should go to the water. Except for 5, who had yet to return, the others gathered and stood at the edge of the easy way to the stream. 4 got to his feet and grunted. The shortest distance to the water required moving backward down a steep shift in the dirt that always sent rocks and dead brush into a tumble. 4 and 5 had done this many times and often slid fast, on purpose. But the larger group always took the easy way to the stream. 1 and 3 at the front, 4 at the back. Always looking, mostly aware. When they arrived, 4 would walk them into the water and continue to the other side to keep an eye on them and the ridge that fronted their cave.

But this time he lingered as they stood ankle-deep in the cold wet.

He couldn't stop staring at the High Place. He knew how the world worked. He did not make mistakes. He was not careless. He had power over dirt and rocks. Controlled them. Not the other way around.

They each lay down in the stream and let it run over and past them. 3 squealed and slapped 1's leg. She rubbed 3's ear and grunted at 6 and 7, who were finding smooth stones in the streambed and casting sullen eyes at 4.

There was a rumble. They couldn't tell from which direction, but all looked toward the High Place, expecting to spot the hot ooze jumping. Seeing no change in activity on those slopes, they soon focused again on the water. The next noise was louder and sharper, then lowered to a growl. There was no mistaking where it came from this time. A long-toothed cat.

6 and 7 dropped their stones and looked in the direction of the cave, cut from view by the steep slope.

1 stood and carried 3 to the bank, gently cooing to him. 6 and 7 rolled out of the stream and crouched behind a couple of stones partially submerged in the wet silt. 4 stayed in the water, letting it continue to wash over him. No fear or confusion. No worry. The air and water that moved across him were one, the black sky and rocks sharing the same space. 4 looked up at the dirty smudge of light and got lost in it. He put his hands on his head and stared until it reached the highest point in the filth above. They all knew their own lives depended on waiting long enough to make sure the beast was finished and gone.

After a time, 4 slowly got to his feet and led them to the easy way from the stream.

They'd all seen this sort of thing before in different forms. 1 had watched 2 fade slowly, the victim of a spider. When 4 and 5 first stumbled across 1 and what was then her cave, the only sign of life that seemed to represent this female was an animated 3 by her side. A rotting 2 lay in a distant corner. 4 mounded dirt over him when 1 finally fell to sleep that first night. For days thereafter, she would scream whenever a spider appeared and splay her fingers in a gesture that magnified this particular danger. After calming down, she would go to the mound and touch it gently.

4 had seen his older females fade and had heard a male scream in the night and never be seen again.

This was what they had to go on.

When nearly at the end of the easy way from the stream, they found the shredded mess that once was 5. He was oddly flat, with most everything that had given him form ripped out, horrifying gashes evidence of long teeth at play. There was one arm near the edge of the slope, but no sign of the other. The dirt around what was left of him was dark and wet. The most shocking part was the face. Eyes half shut, mouth nothing more than a gaping hole. No sparkle, no twist of lips. 3 ran to 5 and vigorously patted his head, which lolled to the side where 4 kneeled.

Some rocks slid down the slope.

4 stumbled the rest of the way to the cave, weak and empty. He stared at the patches of ground that 5 had smoothed over after digging up the voles that no one could see. Everywhere else the dirt was parched and cracked but in these spots it looked fresh, revived. He sensed that something bigger was mixed in. Things, not things. Actions, not actions. What wasn't, but could be. 4 stood in the middle of one of these patches and twisted his feet in the turned soil, willing this new vision to fade. The cave was broken, but he would fix it.

He didn't always make mistakes.

He sometimes had power over dirt and rocks.

4 walked to the cave's entrance and turned to look at the start of the easy way to the stream, where a bit further on 5 was being attended to. Somehow. He grumbled softly and sat hard on the Smooth Stone, throwing his back violently against the wall.

In the moment just before a couple of bird eggs shook free from one of the deep cuts in the wall, landed on 4's head, and ran down his face, he thought of how things would be different. How he would save them. How it would make sense. That they might be lesser for a short time but at least their food would be real.

That was more than possible.

Small Measures

He'd asked the same question four, five times and the seer finally gave the expected and feared answer. He and his kids were going to die. Not tomorrow or the next day. Today. It would be unfair and violent, and the news photos would be raw and uncensored. The how part wasn't clear. Some guy with a knife. Machete, maybe. Indoors, outdoors. Couldn't quite picture that, either. The visionary shrugged and said she didn't make the rules. You see what they let you see and work with it.

He'd never actually visited a seer out in the world, but the dream was very real. It ended with him paying for the information using large bags of rice paraded in on the shoulders of a relentless stream of clowns.

So vivid. Made sense.

He woke sputtering to another sweltering sunrise, pillow stuck to the back of his head, sweat creeping over his scalp's age spots and through remaining wisps of hair. He hadn't worn the breathing apparatus from the VA to help with his sleep apnea for several days in a row. His eyes fixed on the ceramic kangaroo on the dresser past the footboard, only house and shed keys poking from its pouch. Nothing he could use to start the Pontiac. He'd long ago run a jeep at speed past traps and around missing sections of road near Inchon, but the last of his stateside cars now sat beat in the driveway, the victim of a few head-ons. Mailbox, cherry tree, and phone booth.

The latter was the final straw for the authorities. You don't take out historic relics, accident or not. They sent a long rundown of his situation and provided an email address through which to lodge an appeal, thereby effectively putting the matter to an end.

The kangaroo winked.

He closed his eyes again, hoping the seer might still be there to answer one last question. There was nothing for some time, but then a handwritten to-do list materialized. Only one item on it, and that was blurry. Much more time passed before he could just about make out the words.

You know what to do.

He turned his head to look at the other bed in the room. Where the kids lay still. Side by side and on their backs, uncovered because of the heat. The seer's truth burned in a place behind his eyes, which became wet.

Nobody would cut them down today.

But anything could happen at any time and he needed to act fast. He fumbled for the bed remote, arthritic fingers finally finding the cord and reeling it in. The up button was finicky. Sometimes the bed responded quickly and easily, but the usual reaction was a little up, a little down, and often nothing at all. If the machinery cooperated, he could roll out of bed from a nearly sitting position and slide into the slippers he kicked into place every night.

No response from the button. He would get no help today.

It took some rocking back and forth in bed to gain the required momentum to propel his considerable bulk a bit forward and swing to the side. A tricky maneuver that had seen him hit the floor a couple of times. Last time, he lay there nearly all day in his stained t-shirt and incontinence briefs and almost decided to stay down for the count. He needed to look after the kids, though, and that was inspiration enough to crawl to the nightstand between the two beds and pull onto his knees. He cursed himself on that occasion for being neglectful, but they looked as peaceful as ever and that gave no small measure of comfort and strength.

The seer's earlier words gave him the will to put his feet on the floor. He sat hunched on the edge of the bed for a few minutes, hands on knees, regaining breath from the effort. The sun was starting to hit the kids' toes and he didn't want them to burn. With another rocking motion, he hauled onto his feet and used the nightstand to steady himself while he worked toward their bed.

The three girls lay perfectly still. Decades old but small as the day they were born, they needed his care. They were fragile now and could melt in the heat. Two kept their eyes open at all times, and he was worried they weren't entering enough sleep stages to stay healthy. The third's eyes were closed and only opened when he sat her upright, revealing that one was broken and the other fading to white. One of the kids had wet the bed. She was the only one who could do that, and he made sure she got a glass of water every night. He hadn't been able to change the sheets for weeks now, and she lay in a mess of toilet paper he placed under her each day before bedtime. The girl with closed eyes was missing an arm, which the dog, now gone, had ripped from her in an apparent fit of jealousy.

Electrical tape covered the wound. Small holes in her scalp showed where missing hair had been.

He started to speak and choked on the words. Didn't want to give the specifics of what was bound to happen, all four of them to be victims of a madman's blade. Just spoke of love and duty and how being a father was the greatest job he'd ever had. How he'd do anything and everything for them. They were his life. The end would be still and quiet.

Behind him, he could sense the kangaroo winking again.

He finished his declaration and stopped crying. There would be no violence, no news story on victims of carnage. He slowly slid the pillow out from under their heads and set it on the nightstand. Their bodies moved awkwardly while this happened, toppling into each other. He straightened them out, spacing them at one hand width's distance from each other, and kissed their foreheads.

It's not your fault. Never could be. You're perfect.

He placed the pillow over their heads and pressed down just enough. It was difficult to keep his balance, and he used every bit of strength to stay upright. Had to keep them completely safe from a brutal attack. To take his mind off this effort, he sang.

Happy birthday to you. Happy birthday to you.

He got all the way through three times before running out of breath and collapsing onto their bed.

The seer came to him in his darkness and smiled.

That was a close one, she said.

About the Author

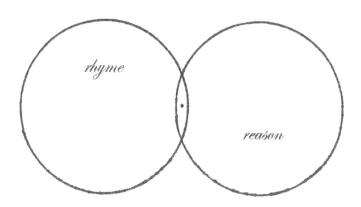

Acknowledgements

Here's to all the misfits, freaks, outsiders, individualists, screwups, and other oddballs. Without you I'd have very little to say.

This book exists because of Rich Perin, whose devotion to the Portland, Oregon writing community is surpassed only by his prodigious skill as a wordsmith. Thanks to Jerry Sampson for massaging my scribblings into much better health.

I'm grateful to all who have helped me approach the status of writer and promise to keep working at it. Special thanks in this regard to Carter Sickels, Whitney Otto, Jon Raymond, Emily Chenoweth, and Margaret Malone.

The following people have provided invaluable support, advice, eyes, and ears: Hobie Anthony, Lisbeth Asay, Ann Beman, Margaret Bloomfield, Karina Brown, Susannah Carver, Eve Connell, Dea-Anne D'Amico, Selene Damard, Meg Devoe, Beth DiPasquale, Ean Eldred, Bobby Eversmann, Richard Garfield, Gerry Gast, Jim Gearhart, Richard Gil, Alisha Gorder, Mare Heron Hake, Sanjay Josse, Sara Kachelman, Carmel Kadrnka, David Kamens, John Kashiwabara, Carol Kekez, Jennifer Leilani Knauss, Leslie Wells Knight, Steve Korbich, Yi Shun Lai, Dylan Lee, Ricky Lee, Ann Litow, Tracey Locke, Jill Murphy Long, Tom Meyer, Jessica Dylan Miele, Amy Foster Myer, Dunja Nedić, Erica Nikolaidis, Rick Nobleman, Kerry Nylen, Peter Nylen, J.P. Paull, Kara Pierce, Jared Polesky, Alan Purkart, the Red House Writers, Jo Sparkes, Christine Toth, Bill Tripp, Ron Waalkes, Maw Shein Win, Raechel Wolfe, Nancy Wong, Blaine Zaid, and Hilary Zaid.

To Tim Sassoon for the being the first to publish one of my tales. Long live *BOX*.

But most of all to Grace M, with whom I live all the best stories.

San Cat

CPSIA information can be obtained
at www.ICGtesting.com
Printed in the USA
FSHW010259070319
56047FS